Ryan is a disillusioned marriage counselor tempted into an enigmatic couple's web of intrigue. To survive, he must confront his failure to live up to his own ideals of honesty and trust and simultaneously reawaken his belief in the redemptive power of love. A delightful post-modern tale... repackaging eternal questions of romance.

David Nel.lo,

Premi Sant Jordi Novelist

Marriage Dance

Patrick Pfister

SPUYTEN DUYVIL

New York City

I am grateful to the following people who read and commented on the manuscript: Carmen Biarnés, Craig Carr, Pamela Field, Susan Hostetler, Jeff Palmer, tt and Terry Wooten.

For Gabrielle Deakin

Chapter One

Today the sun crosses the plane of the earth's equator. The autumn equinox when the moon is mad and the oceans heave. Night and day at equal length over the planet. Harvest time. Winter not yet real.

My cell phone rings. It's Shirley, the receptionist at the Monterey Counseling Center where I have rented a consultation office.

"Beth Dijkstra is here," she says.

"What?" I check my watch. "She's two hours early."

"That's what I told her but she said she'd wait. She's in your office."

"What? What about Malcolm?"

"Who?"

"Malcolm. Her husband."

"There's no husband here."

"Okay, I'm on my way."

What the hell, I think. People nod their heads, say they understand and it turns out they're not even listening. Or maybe they're already divorced.

I stand on the edge of Lovers Point Park in the town of Pacific Grove. In front of me, immense Monterey Bay stretches into the Pacific. Gray whales will soon pass by on their 5,000 mile migration from the Bering Sea to their breeding grounds in Baja. Great ritual drama of perfection through sacrifice.

Morning fog shrouds the sea while kelp forests sway beneath the waves. A squadron of brown pelicans glides in single file, surfing the updraft of a wave face. A few of the pterodactyl-like birds already display mating plumage. They go into a hover and then a wing-tucked kamikaze dive. Their giant, gray bills slice into waves. They flap upward, water spilling from their orange throat pouches. Farther out to sea, spears of sunlight pierce the fog. The pelicans and gleaming spear thrusts dazzle my eyes. For an instant I feel like a butterfly impaled by a fine dart of beauty. How can I behold such majesty and remain blind?

I put my cycling helmet back on and re-mount my new bike. I start pedaling and am soon flying along the coastal path toward Monterey, the wind at my back. I pass the Aquarium and Cannery Row. As Fisherman's Wharf comes into sight, I realize sweat is oozing out of me and I can't go straight to the office. I turn onto Scott but only make it halfway up the hill. Not in shape. I push the bike down Watson Street and come to a yard bordered by purple ice plants, a house with a high brick porch. This, I remind myself, is where I now live.

I shower and dress in a blue sport coat and chinos. The other therapists in the Counseling Center call my clothes "Hollywood duds." All of them, even the women, dress in sweaters and jeans. Everyone in Monterey seems to own fifty sweaters. I need a new wardrobe along with my new bike and rented house.

Walking back down the hill to Fisherman's Wharf, I focus on Beth Dijkstra and Malcolm Favor. We met two weeks ago, a twenty-minute, free-of-charge preliminary session. The morning after I arrived from LA. I was disoriented and debilitated from the long drive followed by a sleepless night, but I clearly remember laying out my ground rules. First rule: I only meet the couple together, never individually. Understood? Both of them nodded, pronounced the word *Yes*. Two mature, intelligent people who understood and agreed. Divorce, I think again. At least they can't blame me for causing it.

A faint rainbow now shimmers above the fog, bridging the heavens from Santa Cruz to Big Sur. I become aware of the chorus of mammals, the ancient song, rumbling and mournful. A purse-seine captain told me that the sea lions kick up the real racket—the prolonged barking cries—and the harbor seals provide the background moans. As I push through the Counseling Center door, the noise of barking sea lions merges into the muffled hum of Reception, of nearby office activity, the photocopy machine clicking and humming.

I nod at Shirley and head down the hall to my office. It contains everything I brought up from LA in the U-Haul, hastily thrown into place before my preliminary session with Beth Dijkstra and Malcolm Favor. The walls hold color photographs of mountains and lakes along with some professional assurance: my MFT titles, certificates from clinical residences and seminars. A weekend workshop at Esalen. An Indian blanket and two pastel watercolors. Safe, warm, cozy. Beyond my desk, three armchairs sit on a circular throw rug, forming a triangle in the center of the room. Beth Dijkstra sits on one of the chairs, a book open on her lap, jotting down a note. She looks academic, absorbed, northern European. Did I think this when we first met? I can't remember. She closes the book, removes her reading glasses, rises from the chair.

"Hello, Ryan," she says.

Her voice betrays a quaver. In her mid-to-late thirties, she wears a flower print dress and coral cashmere sweater. She has what used to be called dishwater blond hair, a disheveled mop of it. I take her hand in mine. Her palm is warm, slightly damp. No wedding ring on her left hand. Did she wear one in the preliminary session? Can't remember that either.

We sit. By force of habit, I enter a state of heightened receptivity, at ease yet intensely alert. I become aware of her posture and respiration rate, a tightness in her neck, a flutter above her jaw line.

"Are you all right?" I ask.

"I'm trying to be."

I feel emotions scattering her thoughts. The depth of her in-breath alters, her skin tone pales.

"I'm afraid we won't be needing your services after all," she says.

I reply in a neutral tone: "I had thought our preliminary session went well."

"It went very well," she says. "You see, Malcolm—he's the one, he's… not well. It started… in his shoulder."

"His shoulder?"

"His right shoulder but then it turned out to be his liver. They call it 'referral pain'."

I show no sign of perplexity but my fingers raise an inch off the chair arm, urging her on. She speaks faster and I have the impression of a prepared account disintegrating into a litany of medical terms. A liver ultrasound scan, two blood tests, an MRI, hepatic arteriography. "Now they say…" She hesitates. "…last week, I mean. Now they say *terminal*."

I let a moment pass. As an afterthought, she adds that two specialists have confirmed the diagnosis. Her blue-green eyes hold me in a steady gaze. Deep emotions sway inside her, like the kelp forests in the Bay. I sense a cave, submerged and shadowed. She hides something there. Maybe herself.

"The terrible irony," she continues, "is that it instantly put marital distress on a back burner."

I glance at the third armchair. In twenty years I have never sat in this triangle of chairs with only one other person. It feels strange, unnatural. I'm compelled to include the empty chair in our conversation.

"How is Malcolm?" I ask.

"Stoic," she answers. "Or stunned. I'm not sure which. Maybe he's one and I'm the other."

"Is he in pain?"

She shakes her head. "Low level at the moment. He takes some Ibuprofen." She pauses for a breath. "So the reason I came today…"

"Yes?"

"… is that we no longer need your services for our marriage, but he needs you."

"I don't understand," I say, but my hands understand. They tremble on the chair arms.

"He says a year might pass before he finds another therapist like you. Two years. Right now he doesn't have two days to waste."

I shake my head slowly, carefully. "Beth, I'm sorry. Truly sorry. But I'm simply not qualified. It's way out of my area. Far from helping, I might do Malcolm—and you—a serious disservice. Besides, we've only had one preliminary session and it's not enough to…"

"It is for Malcolm. He believes you listen well and care deeply." She is silent for a beat and then adds on impulse: "I find you noble."

I sit motionless. To affirm or deny would be less than noble. I feel trapped, obliged from this moment on to act noble before her. Still, my newfound nobility doesn't stop me from thinking that I can't afford to lose any clients. I discern the shadowed cave driving her to insist.

"It wasn't only the first session," she says. "We've watched your workshop talks at Esalen."

"You mean on YouTube?" The long ago and far away. I'm surprised anyone still clicks on them.

"Malcolm wouldn't ask you to perform miracles. Only to help keep the darkness at bay. So no expectations. He has the hospital, the doctors and nurses and all the support groups for that."

I feel like the walls and dual pane window, the ceiling and floor vacuum-pack an air bubble. Insisting to get her way doesn't come easy for her. She has to force the words out.

"But he also wants someone private and personal," she says. "He says in his heart he knows that person is you."

"I'm sorry, Beth, profoundly sorry that I can't help. I only wish I could."

Her blue-green eyes light up. She knows she has penetrated the barrier of my resistance.

"Please think about it," she says. "Whatever you decide, I'd like to ask you to come out to Pacific House and visit. It would mean a lot to Malcolm."

We rise from the armchairs. I walk her down the hall past Reception, shake her hand. Still warm, but no longer damp. We bid each other goodbye. Back in my office, I linger near the door absorbing the silence, the presence clients leave behind after a session. What was she reading that so enthralled her? I didn't see the cover but I sense it was intellectual, scholarly. On the brink of divorce, husband with terminal cancer—anybody else would stare blankly into space yet she was busily taking notes. Once again my eye goes to the third armchair. Still empty, except for a tremor.

I open the window, lean onto the sill and look out at the harbor. Misted air trickles over my face, smelling of seaweed. Above the fog bank, the rainbow is still faint. I listen to the sea lions, their ancient song, rumbling and mournful. I recall my earlier thoughts. The equinox. Harvest time. Winter not yet real.

Chapter Two

The night is quiet, the night is endless. I roll out of bed and head for the kitchen. Unaccustomed to the house in the dark, I extend my arm, wave it in front of me, creep down the hallway. The kitchen clock says 3:21 AM. I turn on the tap, run water into a glass, take a sip. I still hear or imagine I hear the ancient song. The night is not so quiet after all. Do sea lions sleep? Maybe the sound I hear is their snoring.

I should be snoring as well, but Beth Dijkstra's words still run through my head. *I find you noble.* How in the name of six oceans did she ever *find* that? Strange way of putting it too. Why not say, *I think you are noble* or *You seem noble to me.* In any case, the path to nobility is simple. All you have to do is act noble. Only that. She even explained how to do it: by keeping the darkness at bay.

The daytime reflections of nocturnal man. Wake up, I think, and go back to sleep. Maybe I am sleeping and it only seems like I am thinking. I told her I was unqualified, didn't I? I made it very clear. She can have no doubts; besides, I have enough of those for both of us. Maybe I should also have told her that I am not noble at all, no matter how she may find me. I am very *unnoble.* Is that even a word? No, it isn't; the word is *ignoble,* but does *ig* mean the same as *un?* I doubt it. Another doubt.

I should be sleeping but I am awake and dreaming. I am not well. I know it. I should be the one seeing a therapist. I am infected. The world is infected. Man and woman, candle and flame, seed and soil. Core union has come undone. I have seen too much slipshod alchemy, listened to too many tattered tales of wedded woe. He said this and then he did that. She said she loved me but then she didn't. If only everyone would quiet down. If only they would chew on their own words and see if they can swallow them. They can't, of course, so they want me to chew, swallow and even digest. My only cure for their disquiet is to remember they don't know any better.

Have I made a mistake? I believed it would be enough just to get out of LA, that city of devils whose pitchforks took aim at my heart. That city whose own heart thumps like a cheap sound effect. Escape was my vain dream, or maybe my own trivial drama. Why did I choose Monterey and not Boston, Dallas or Sacramento? Was it because of a great love of Steinbeck or a lifelong interest in marine biology? Did I want to spend the remainder of my years kayaking, whale watching, playing golf? No, none of that. I can't even say I wanted to get away from the traffic, pollution, crime, racism, homelessness, obesity, phoniness and earthquakes. No, I wanted a new location that, by coincidence, was very close to an old location where, years ago, someone might truly have said, *I find you noble.* I have returned to the scene of my nobility.

But I am polarized. Like everyone else, I oppose myself. I must transmute rotten fruit into seed. I must learn to see anew. I take another sip of water and pour myself into the sink, empty myself into a dark drain. I leak and gurgle down through clogged valves and pipes. Descending matter, ascending spirit. Somewhere they meet. Somewhere fruit decays into new seed. In the fruition of past effort, the seed may be found.

Far ago and long away, I once upon a crime believed in alchemy. I believed the feminine and masculine could intertwine and weave duality into a union approaching the divine. The twin flame exists. That much I know, that much I believe. Or once believed. Light and darkness truly balanced. Not mere change, but transmutation. How to rock your solitude and stay footloose in a mad whirling dance; that's the question.

I creep back down the dark hallway, again waving my arm in front of me. Groping in the dark. Exactly the nuptial path, exactly life's path. Hopeful, blind, on collision course. My fingertips touch the door, nudge it aside. I cross the room, find the bed. I sit on the edge still thinking daytime thoughts. Some day I will see again. I will experience insight, revelation, epiphany. For now, I slip under the coverlet and lie still. The night is endless, the night is quiet.

CHAPTER THREE

The dawn of a new day. That's what they say and that's what I want to believe. Everything changes. A new beginning on a new foundation. Leaving LA and planting myself like a seed in fertile land wasn't enough. I hunger for a new role, hunger to re-embody energy in a new act. I'm the one who needs to keep darkness at bay.

When Beth referred to their residence as "Pacific House," I didn't think much of it. Cute names instead of geographical addresses adorn all the fairy-tale cottages in Carmel-by-the-Sea. Heavenly Villa. Gentle Zephyr. On a Cloud. I assumed Pacific House in nearby Pebble Beach would be yet another quaint though costly chalet, but I arrive at a palace on priceless oceanfront property. A chain link fence runs around rolling land. At the main gate a uniformed guard steps out of a small cabin, checks me in and raises an automatic barrier gate arm. As I drive along a lane bordered by purple ice plant, I wonder why Beth and Malcolm ever came to see me in the first place. They could have hired some famous San Francisco psychiatrist to fly down here by helicopter.

Beth welcomes me at the front door. She looks into my eye and smiles gratitude but her thoughts are elsewhere. Or she would like to be elsewhere. She guides me through rooms and hallways vectoring off in all directions. We pass a sunroom with a yellow chaise lounge, a small library appointed with postmodernist chairs and come to a billiard room, where a maid flicks a duster over marble statuary. Beth introduces her as Yetta. She explains that Yetta is Romanian and speaks French but not much English. Beth addresses her in what seems to me perfect French and then says Yetta will guide me out after my meeting with Malcolm. Good, because if I have to find my own way, I won't arrive home until next week.

Some unspoken worry passes between the two women. Then Beth leads me onward down another corridor. Expensive artwork on the walls. Strange place. Half mansion, half museum. Doric capitals crown the pilasters on the portal to the west wing. Finally, we arrive at a large kitchen and dinette. Ceiling-high windows look out on a rolling yard and the ocean beyond. Beth pulls open a sliding glass door and gestures toward the horizon.

"Malcolm is down by the point," she says.

Her blue-green eyes encase me in warmth and appreciation, but she is anxious to get away. From me or the house or herself, I can't tell which. Tics, gestures, facial twitching, short breaths and muscle tightening used to compose the vocabulary of my own perfect foreign language. My intuition, my powers of observation, were once so fluent I could read and interpret any mannerism. Now all I can do is catch myself trying to act noble in front of her.

"Thank you so much, Ryan," she says, and means it.

She turns and hurries off and I start across the yard. Ocean breeze billows my sport coat, tosses my hair. I angle toward the outcropping of a headland. Thirty yards off to my left, a Mexican gardener on his hands and knees labors at the earth, digging a trowel into a flower bed. I feel I am like him, like Yetta the maid. A hired hand arriving to work. Most therapists ask clients their profession. I rarely do. What does it matter if someone suffering marital grief is a lawyer, a cook, a plumber? Still, I can't help but wonder where all this comes from.

The land ends where a twenty-foot precipice drops into the Pacific. Malcolm stands near a flat granite boulder, tall and rangy, his carved cheeks ruddy. His projected good health strikes me as odd, as if he's trying to hide the weakness the cancer has inflicted on him. In his right hand he holds a cane with a pearl handle in the shape of an eagle's beak. His step falters and he quickly re-positions the cane. He doesn't actually stumble but the nearby cliff edge worries me.

Like me, he is in his early forties. Black, unblinking eyes. As with Beth, I can't picture him in my office sitting in the triangle of armchairs. A hazy memory of remote emotion, like tiny bubbles popping. Nothing clear-cut. I should have reviewed my notes before coming out here. Where was I that day of the preliminary session— how did I not see him? Yet now I am conscious of his commanding presence, his hyper-vigilant gaze. Down below, the breakers are white and thunderous. Farther west, tendrils of black fog hang above the waves. Malcolm brandishes his cane at the raging sea.

"Savage, lawless nature," he says. "In all her glory."

We walk along the cliff edge. He turns his large head toward me, his gaze still dark. Maybe it wasn't Beth who wanted to get away; maybe it was me. I am out of my depth entering my spurious new role. Still, I determine that I will not vex him with stock phrases. *I'm sorry to hear you're going through this. How do you feel? How long have the doctors given you?* But then he catches me off guard with his own question:

"Do you know what deer eat?"

He has spoken as if we've been discussing animal diets for the last hour. I grow acutely aware that I have never counseled any seriously ill client. Not only out of my depth, but sinking fast.

"I'm not sure," I reply. "Berries, leaves...?"

"Yes, berries and leaves. They also eat plants, bone meal, fruit trees, conifers, perennials, and all forms of garbage. They consume entire orchards and nurseries. They eat everything you can imagine and everything you can't. They are innocent only in appearance."

I nod, letting him talk. The crashing surf and ocean roar are distracting. We should be in a quiet room in the house. I look back across the yard at Pacific House and he follows my line of vision.

"Impressive, isn't it?" he says. "As a young architect, I could only dream of such a dwelling."

His gaze ignites violently, as if the house itself has burst into flames, but he turns back to me so quickly I think I have imagined it. I wonder if he is the designer and builder of Pacific House.

"Beth told me you wanted to continue our sessions," I say, "but re-focus them to meet present needs."

He wiggles his cane, contemplates the tip.

"First, I have questions," he says. "To begin with, what will these re-focused sessions do for me?"

"Beth mentioned that you hoped they might afford you some peace of mind."

"And will they?"

"I can't answer that."

"Then I'll be more precise: what will you do for me in these re-focused sessions?"

"For starters, I'll listen."

"Listen to what?"

"Whatever you have to say."

"Even if I ramble on about hungry deer and Mother Nature?"

He speaks with apparent humor but I detect something more serious. Perhaps denial or anger. Either would be normal for a man recently diagnosed with cancer, but I sense constriction, the jagged edge of an icy will, a psyche out of balance.

"Even that," I answer lightly. "And if you don't feel like talking, we can listen to the wind and waves."

He studies me for a moment and then says: "My wife

and I watched you speaking at Esalen." He flourishes the cane again, points it southward in the direction of Big Sur. "I followed all three of your talks with great interest. 'The Alchemical Marriage,' 'Psyche and Eros' and 'Twin Soul or Twin Flame'."

"I gave those talks a long time ago." Back when I was noble.

"But Esalen and YouTube keep them alive in the mainstream. I wonder how you came to choose the three topics."

The ocean roar continues to annoy me, or perhaps I am annoyed by my new role. The man is dying and I'm glibly trying to reinvent myself. Like the surf crashing across the shore rocks, our conversation sprays out rampantly.

"They formed part of a weekend workshop I gave," I say. "The topics evolved out of articles I had written on alchemy in relationships."

"You described the possibility of 'transformational radiance' in marriage. I liked that phrase. But did Esalen limit you to three topics or did you decide on the number three yourself?"

Strange question. "I don't really remember. Why do you ask?"

"Because the ancient Greeks considered Three to be the perfect number. It is the number of Time: past, present, future. It is the number of existence: birth, life, *death*." He pauses, looks away, looks back at me.

"Recalling the three armchairs in your office, it occurred to me that you always form part of a triad. If we begin our re-focused sessions, it will just be the two of us. You and me."

Curious that he should say this because I strongly sense the presence of some third entity. Beth, Pacific House, the cancer—I'm not sure what, but it is here. Beneath us, foam and spray continue to wash over the shore rocks. The black fog still rides the crest of the breakers. Is this the new foundation I seek? I weigh my words, speak carefully.

"That occurred to me also," I say. "It simply means I'll have to change my focus."

Simply? How smoothly that word rolled off my tongue. He stops walking and turns toward me, shaking his large head yet maintaining his gaze.

"We all meet death alone," he says. "It's a trite sentiment, but nonetheless true. True no matter how well or poorly married we might be." He pauses a beat. "Which brings me to a final question. Will you be with me all the way?"

I stare into his black eyes, thinking that a new role should be given to a pioneer, an innovator. No cycle repeats itself, but what if it is not just new, but my true role, my dharma? All the same, it's still an old pledge, one I know well. *In sickness and health, until death do we part.*

I resolve that I must act significantly. I raise my voice above ocean roar, "I'll be there."

CHAPTER FOUR

A banner headline in the *Herald* reads "A Whale of a Day!" and a color photo shows five humpbacks lunging skyward, their great maws agape, water streaming off extended throat pleats. The newspaper reports 15,000 Sooty Shearwater birds wheeling and diving above the underwater canyon. In addition to the whales, 500 sea lions and 2,000 Long Beaked Common Dolphins join the lunge feeding, a multi-species aggregate banquet so densely packed it creates a churning cauldron of fins, water and beating wings.

Later, a television news team interviews a drag boat deck hand who conjectures that "a large concentration of krill, sardines and anchovies sparked the frenzy." At the end of the report, a second interview features an old salt in a battered yacht captain's hat, who winks at the camera and says, "Ain't no stink worse than whale breath." Then he grins, tips his hat and shouts, "Whale ahoy!"

If I needed convincing, the event makes it clear I am no longer a resident of the City of Angels, no longer stuck in throbbing traffic amid massive urban sprawl. In LA, the ocean defines a limit, keeping a mammoth metropolis somewhat sane. Here in Monterey, the ocean proclaims magnificence. Pedaling along the coast on my new bike, I enter realms of majesty and splendor, freedom and deliverance. I arch my spine, lean forward onto the handlebars, pedal harder, faster.

I stop at a used bookstore on Lighthouse Avenue and buy *On Death and Dying* by Kübler-Ross, a manual entitled, *Death Therapy: A Journey of Compassion* and a third text by a Tibetan *rimpoche*. Back home, paging through the books, I no longer feel an intimate of magnificence. Rather, I feel growing unease. I review things I said to Malcolm. I think of things I should have said. I must remind myself that I have been treating souls in despair for many years. The couples who come to see me are in pain and suffering. No, they are not dying, but many feel like they are. They writhe and ache and gasp for breath. Malcolm needs basic human kindness, someone to bear witness to his suffering and validate his pain. He needs affection, needs to engage transition and release regret.

No matter the effort I make, I can't summon a clear memory of our preliminary session. I was too tired, too disoriented by the long drive and relocation. However, afterwards in the silence of my office, as always, I jotted down my impressions. Now I consult the notes I should have read yesterday before going out to Pacific House.

Beth Dijkstra: practical perfectionist. Artistic temperament. Warm, wounded, possible manic depressive tendency. Speaks directly to me yet somehow to another, perhaps her father. Religious impulse. Intuition hampered by overly active mind. Dedicated, erudite, romantic.

Malcolm Favor: Commanding demeanor. Reserved, assaulted by random thought. Tight shoulder muscles. Possibly ironic. Intelligence like armor minus the chink. Fears tenderness. Black eyes emit glints of chaos. Powerful man. Deeply injured. Proud atheist. Bleak soul.

Added note: What freakish conjunction of heavenly bodies brought this man and woman together?

Like most teens, I rebelled against my parents, not against their authority or to assert my independence, not even because raging hormones were on the loose. I rebelled against their dysfunctional marriage. In my eyes, they betrayed romance and desecrated love. I hated the constant shouting, the plates smashing into walls, hated Mom's pills and Dad's booze. Then came the affairs, the pretending, the stereotype and hypocrisy—I hated all of it. So I rebelled by getting married myself. At age seventeen. My bride was six months younger. Unsurprisingly, she came from a broken home. We separated after a few months, got back together for a while and then celebrated our first anniversary by divorce. Thank all the stars above my star-filled head, we didn't have a child but Dad was still right when he declared, "So Mr. Know-It-All fucks up his life big time."

My life still had a long way to go but I was marked and I wasn't the only one. Two other apples eventually hit the ground near the same tree. My older brother Teddy, now living in Norman, Oklahoma, is on his third shaky marriage. My divorced sister Theresa in Idaho has given up on "the whole charade" and refuses to even go out on a date. Of course, Mom and Dad in Arizona recently celebrated their 47th Anniversary, still together, still throwing plates.

Soon after my divorce, I was accepted into the clinical psychology program at UCLA and granted a student loan. Still Mr. Know-It-All, I barged into academic life demanding upgrades in both theory and practice, and argued with anything my professors tried to teach. As a result, years passed before I attracted a mentor, but the long wait brought gold. Harry Higby, MFT-licensed therapist, marriage and family expert and all-round good guy, became my supervisor for my 3000-hour internship. Under his gentle wing, I worked hard, studied like a fanatic and began to impose my own theories onto Imago Relationship Therapy, the Gottman Method and EFT. Harry managed to tame my wildness yet still encourage my wild ideas. With his support, I eventually founded my own website. The Marriage Dance with Ryan Mattheison.

Activity was slow at first but when I started to publish articles on mythological couples—Psyche and Eros, Tristan and Iseult, Odysseus and Penelope, Orpheus and Eurydice—hits on the site increased. Excerpts from my articles were referenced, reprinted or quoted on other sites. I corresponded with other marriage therapists and participated in online discussion panels devoted to "marriage in modern times." Then Harry suggested that I take a look at the Esalen Residence Program. He thought my "vision" would fit right into the "Esalen universe."

So I studied the Esalen guidelines, which recommended a "deep understanding and level of experience," but didn't require extensive presentation skills. An ability to "create a safe space" so that guests could learn was "paramount." Topics might be general or specific but needed to align with the Esalen mission. Esalen even encouraged proposals from people who were "new to teaching" and wanted to "hone in on their passions and clarify their thinking."

I decided I had nothing to lose, so I filled out an application and submitted a proposal for a ten-hour weekend workshop entitled "The Marriage Dance." Harry might have put in a good word, but if so, he never mentioned it. In any case, my proposal was accepted.

The fog comes and goes in wisps, sculpting cypress pines, crowning kelp beds. Some days at Lovers Point the lacy mist thickens into cloud. I squeeze the hand brakes and roll to a stop at El Carmelo Cemetery. The graves run in flat rows, flagstone paths bridging the Underworld. To the west, Point Pinos Lighthouse stands tall and resolute; gulls circle the beacon, screeching. A herd of deer, perhaps twenty in all, graze among the tombstones and cenotaphs. They are blacktail and mule deer, the locals say. I'm still unable to tell the difference, but I recall Malcolm's words about their diets. Looking at the graves, I wonder if he has selected his own final resting place.

A man and woman pass by, speaking in lowered voices. Instinctively, I take two steps back, pulling the bike with me. The universe conspires to set couples in my path. I run into them everywhere. In supermarkets, malls, boardwalks, gas station convenience stores. Snippets of their private marital drama always reach my ears. Rarely do I overhear genuine exchange or even cheerful pillow talk. More often, their murmured endearments foreshadow strife. Soon, I think, they will be flinging desperate emails at my website or stumbling teary eyed into my consultation office. The man and woman are almost out of earshot when I overhear the woman say, "...but I don't want to."

At least the background chorus has changed. The angry snarl of LA traffic has become a serenade of wind and sea. Somehow the serenade contains the honeyed gallantry of courtship. Now even the cries of killdeer and snowy plover sound like bill and coo. Monterey lays pink sand verbenas and yellow beach poppies beyond my front wheel, luring me out of my frazzled LA self.

I pedal southwest onto Sunset Drive, ride along Spanish Bay and finally stop at Asilomar State Beach. My face is damp with sweat and mist. Fog shrouds the Pacific from shore to horizon. A few people walk dogs on the beach. A whippet chases a Frisbee. Off to the left, a dozen young people huddle around a campfire. Is it legal to build a fire here? From the distance I can't distinguish if they are talking, singing or sitting in silence, but the scene reminds me of the couple I saw a few minutes ago. I used to think of a couple as the first unit of community, used to think a couple might form the core of an urge to create a new society, the dawning communion of new values. If two souls can't get along, then how can three or four? Around the fire of common dedication, I once wrote on my web page, people commune; they become a shared chalice receiving inspiration. But only if a central flame burns.

In LA, I never would have accepted the Garcias as clients. A bit too ordinary for my refined tastes, I suppose, but long lines of troubled couples no longer knock at my door. Until my finances recover, I will welcome whoever walks into my office. Later that afternoon, starting our first session, Mr. Garcia says, "I sure never thought I'd be sitting on a couch with a shrink."

"Just to be clear," I reply, "I'm a therapist, not a psychiatrist. And it's an armchair, not a couch."

"Everyone knows an armchair is just a small couch," Mr. Garcia counters.

"Well, I'm not a shrink."

He shrugs. "Okay, if you say so."

Mrs. Garcia throws me a look, as in *See what I have to swallow?* For the next hour I act like a referee at a mudslinging match. Afterwards, I announce that we have made good progress.

"Nobody makes progress in a marriage," Mr. Garcia says. "The minute you say *I do,* you put the car in Reverse and start rolling back downhill."

I walk them out of the office. As we head through Reception, my eye goes to the Waiting Area. Beth Dijkstra sits there, pen in hand, an open book once again on her lap. I bid the Garcias goodbye. Beth puts the pen and book into her purse, removes her glasses, gets to her feet. I lower my voice:

"Beth, I think I told you I only see a couple together, never separately."

"I remember," she says. "But Malcolm said you had agreed that the new sessions would only involve the two of you." Her unlined brow describes relief. "So now I'm the third wheel out of the picture."

"You're right," I say. "I forgot."

"He wanted me to give you this."

She extracts an envelope from her purse. I think she is delivering a message of some sort but my fingertips encounter thickness. I pull back the flap and find a wad of fifty dollar bills.

"Malcolm always pays in cash," she explains.

"But this is too much..."

"He calculated the time you would spend driving out

to Pacific House..." Her tone of voice makes me wonder if she still lives there. "And the hours you might be taking away from other clients. If it's a problem of any kind, you can always talk to him."

"No, no," I say. "I'm just surprised, that's all. It's unusual... but much appreciated."

It also seals the deal. No backing out now. I better dive into my self-help books as fast as possible. I don't know what to do with the envelope. Why didn't Malcolm just give it to me tomorrow in our next session? In LA, nobody except a drug dealer or maniac would carry around so much cash. I feel like I'm committing an illegal act. Finally, I stuff it into the inner pocket of my sport coat.

"I was just on my way out the door," I say. How long has she been waiting here?

We walk out into the chorus of moaning sea lions. The wharf is full of tourists. The lunge feeding of the other day has brought excited crowds to the whale watching tours. One sign reads, "The Whales Arrive Early This Year!"

"I'm going to have a look at the harbor," Beth says. It is both statement of intent and tacit invitation. "I haven't been down the Wharf in a long while."

As we stroll past the whale watchers, I feel the nudge of the envelope against my ribs. Like a nervous tourist, I keep checking to make sure the bundle hasn't disappeared or dropped through my pocket onto the boardwalk. I ask about Malcolm and Beth says he is still apparently without pain although he sometimes experiences a tingling sensation in his chest. The way she says *apparently* rings off key. I don't know why. I remind myself that she is no longer my client. I haven't yet asked how far Malcolm's cancer has metastasized. The book by the Tibetan *rimpoche* recommends that I don't fixate or become hooked on medical detail. I have a terminally ill client. That's all I need to know.

We arrive at the end of the pier and look out over the yachts and fishing boats. I find I have nothing more to say. I don't feel like making small talk and it seems she doesn't either. We stand side by side watching a blue-gray harbor seal pass by in the water beneath us. Our shared silence is pleasant, perhaps because the song of the sea lions fills it.

"What's that line by Kerouac?" Beth murmurs. "The seals break my heart with their coughing cries of love...'"

I look at her. If she wants to impress me, she has. But her expression is relaxed, her thoughts already elsewhere. So the quote was neither feat of magic nor big ego on display, just a familiar phrase plucked out of everyday memory.

The fog hovers above the becalmed bay and the sea lions go on barking. A minute later Beth says, "It's nice to see you again... and now I should go."

CHAPTER FIVE

I have always assumed that Esalen accepted my workshop proposal to fill a scheduling need, or because Harry Higby contacted some event planner. Their lack of review and case analysis still surprises me, but I have to admit that my workshop dovetailed well with other talks given at that time. So a door cracked open and I slipped in.

For the first time in a dozen years, I click on the YouTube link. "The Marriage Dance: A Workshop with Ryan Matheisson." Immediately, I am struck by my youthful appearance: wide open blue eyes, unlined face, scraggly hair, second hand blazer and stonewashed jeans. No Hollywood duds in sight. I appear at ease, like a great teacher about to reveal the foundation of an inner knowledge upon which a new world can be built. Yet I remember trembling as I was introduced, sweating as I faced the audience. I didn't even realize someone was filming. Stage fright, to say the least.

I had expected the large white room at Esalen to offer an academic setting, bookish intellectuals and scholars taking notes. Now I can even imagine Beth Dijkstra sitting there scribbling onto a pad. Instead, the audience was laid back and cool. The lounge area of a discotheque. Guests, seminarians, staff and faculty members sprawled over large cushions, stretched out or sitting half lotus on the floor. One figure stood quietly at the back of the room. Harry Higby urging me on. Outside, the ocean hurled waves at the rocky coastline.

I watch myself smile and thank the presenter for her introduction. I exude a certain callow charm, as if I believe "my vision" is my own and not borrowed from Gottman, Eggerichs, Rilke and a dozen others. My voice is modulated and matter-of-fact if somewhat tremulous, balanced by tones of enthusiasm and conviction in what I say. Enthralled and embarrassed, I continue watching as I launch into my fabled workshop:

"Alchemical marriage is symbolized by the King and Queen, Yin and Yang, divine polar opposites coming together not unlike the left and right hemispheres of the brain. We aspire toward holy alliance, a semi-divine state in which chaos is transmuted into symbiotic union."

The scene cuts to the audience. Some backroom Esalen editor probably smoking high grade product has been creative. The screen shows an attractive long-haired couple recumbent on comfy cushions. They share a kiss. Cut back to me as I go on talking. I still look like a great teacher who through long experience has reached solid and illuminating truths and is now transmitting seed ideas. Perhaps it was mere knowledge disguised as luminous wisdom, but I am still transfixed by my sincerity and faith in myself.

The demon of technology, I think. Triumphs and failures, no matter how great, used to be nothing but passing events; now a computer screen enshrines this: a rash and reckless soul seeking truth. How dare I scold myself for dream and courage, for borrowing a vision. All visions are borrowed. Better if I ask where the vision went, how I ever managed to lose it.

I can't watch any more. I turn off the computer and stare out the window at the Bay. Soon after Esalen, I moved out from under Harry's wing and began a start-up practice in a working class neighborhood of San Diego where I labeled myself a "family counselor." A couple of years later, Esalen invited me back to give a follow-up workshop on "the same thrilling theme," but I never replied. Later, I moved to LA and reincarnated as a "marriage therapist." Now in Monterey, I seek a new incarnation, a new vision.

I arrive at Pacific House the following day, this thought still in mind. Yetta the Romanian maid greets me at the door and guides me down the long corridors. I ask how she is but she smiles shyly as we pass the sunroom, the library, the billiard room. I leave her in the kitchen and start across the rolling yard. Once again, the gardener is digging at a flower bed. Near the cliff edge by the flat granite boulder, Malcom sits on a wicker lawn chair. Behind him, a belt of red cloud buckles the horizon. As I stride across the rutted earth, my adrenals kick in and start pumping. Not so different from taking the stage at Esalen. I feel the weight of my new role. I must rise to the occasion, play my part, strive to see again. Two sandpipers spin out of the cypress grove. Their calls ride the wind, pierce the ocean roar. *Peet-weet. Peet-weet.*

"There is something I want to tell you," Malcolm says even before I greet him, "and I would like you to tell my wife."

He gestures toward the granite boulder. I sit and give him my full attention. His black eyes stare at me unblinkingly. He looks like a cornered animal, not prey but a predator about to turn the tables.

"I have been downgraded," he says. "From years to months to weeks."

I hesitate. "You're speaking medically?"

"Once the doctors begin poking around, they always find something and, sure enough, they have located a malfunctioning aorta. They say my terminal cancer precludes any kind of intervention and vice versa. A diagnosis that puts me between the hammer and the anvil."

A gust of wind or an indrawn breath catches in my throat. "I remember Beth said... you had experienced a tingling sensation in your chest."

"It has turned out to be more than a tingle."

He is dressed in a black sweater and dark pants and holds the eagle's beak cane in his hand. His silver hair stands on end like wire, unruffled by the wind. His complexion is still so hale and pink-cheeked I can't stop from making a trite comment:

"But... you look so healthy."

"And I experience only minor pain," he replies bitterly. "Something I've pointed out to both the cardiologist and the oncologist. Regrettably, they concur it is not uncommon. They say some patients maintain a certain glow until one day without warning the glow snuffs out. A rosy sunset blanketed by dark night. The cardiologist described all this in brutal detail as he stifled yawns. I suppose he was overdue for his afternoon nap."

I look at the sea. The booming depths of blue water. The tide is high but has begun to ebb. Breakers roil across the cove, washing over rocks, leaving slicks of light. I am prepared for anger or frustration, even hopelessness—in a sense I get them every day—but this is a broken iceberg. The tip shows, the fragmented mass is rising. What have I gotten myself into? I recall telling him that if he doesn't feel like talking, we can listen to the wind and waves. Now we are doing exactly that and the noise is deafening.

"So I want you to relay this news to my wife," he says.

I come to my senses, shake my head. "I'm sorry, Malcolm, but you need to do that yourself, no matter how difficult it may be."

"I've tried a half dozen times." He tightens his grip on the eagle's beak. "And I can't bring myself to utter a word. It's why I ask it of you. My wife is not a well woman and I fear it will pierce her like a dagger thrust."

"Not well?"

"I'm aware of the impression she makes. Especially on men. She dazzles quietly. But beneath that quiet dazzle is a troubled mind. You must have noticed. I'm no expert but I suspect she is severely bipolar. Again and again she has refused to seek help. She self medicates with whatever pills she can get her hands on. Marriage counseling was the only way I could get her into any kind of therapy."

I listen without comment but the skin on my backbone prickles. Ten minutes into my new incarnation and I already need rebirth. I want out. Nowhere in the self-help manuals have I read anything like this.

"I'll have to give it some thought," I murmur.

"I appreciate it," he replies. "More than you can imagine."

I shift positions on the boulder, look at the sea, look back at him. Where is truth? The truth within the healer saluting in true humility the truth within the patient. I need to get our talk onto safe ground. I must evoke some process of transmission and what is transmitted can't be mere knowledge. I've never been with only one client. I feel the lack of a third person, yet the lack is overpowered by an even greater presence. The triangle is still formed, but now by me, my client and the raging sea. I search for words.

"A heart condition on top of cancer seems so..."

"Unnecessary?" Malcolm says.

"Illness of any sort violates our sense of fairness..." I

can't keep my mouth shut; my disquiet urges me on. "...
our sense of justice, and two unwelcome diagnoses in
such a short time makes you wonder if—"

"If God is testing me Job fashion?"

"Well, something like that." *Be quiet now,* I warn
myself, but then go on uselessly talking. "If it gives
any comfort, pain is like everything else. Temporary. It
doesn't last."

He regards me closely. "You say it like you are
describing some tender mercy life bestows upon us."

Beneath us a wave molds onto the curl of a rock face,
then flows off it. "I suppose it is a mercy," I say. "Because
without it life would be unendurable."

"Yes..." Malcolm levers a forlorn gaze onto the
sea. "And now I must consider how best to endure the
precious time I have left."

"There must be places you'd like to see," I suggest.
"Experiences you'd like to have."

"Such as?"

In shock, I realize he is speaking facetiously, stringing
me along, laughing inwardly. He has served up a cliché
on a platter and I have swallowed it. Now he chuckles.
The conversation is a big joke.

"I wouldn't know the answer to that," I say. My voice
is flat, but I'm shaken.

"Well, what 'experiences' did you have in mind?" He
begins to smile. "Give me an example of one of these
wonderful experiences you think I should have."

I fend aside his aggression and open my heart. "Have you ever cried for joy?"

His smile fades and his black eyes grow small and hard. "What?"

"Cried for joy. Have you ever shed tears out of pure happiness? I can't imagine leaving life without having done it."

By chance or instinct, I've hit a nerve. The corner of his mouth hooks upward as his right eye squints shut.

"What is this," he says, "some kind of New Age babble to heal the inner child? If so, it'll only make me sicker than I already am. Instead of crying for my own joy, I prefer to laugh at someone else's tragedy."

I look down at a patch of beach at the base of the cliff. The two sandpipers from the cypress grove have alighted there and are wobbling across the mottled sand on thin legs. Years ago I learned not to control a session. Better to take gentle hold of the rudder and steer a course between my own doubt and a client's anxiety. I have also been dutifully studying Kubler-Ross's death model, but is this the Denial or the Anger stage? I caution myself to let the man's rage wash over me like the sea over the rocks below. Still, my vow to bring him peace of mind has been jolted. The other day I considered that his psyche was out of balance. Now I wonder if it is out of balance to the point of psychopathology.

"Listen to the thunder," he says, pointing his cane at the ocean. "Observe the force. Stare at that monolithic reality for a single minute, and you cannot help but come to one conclusion. You are at *its* mercy. If in the next second the wind blows, the waves rise or lightning strikes, you will be dead. Very dead. You are at the whim and mercy of stupid chance. Your so-called joy depends entirely on that thunder. Are you listening?"

"I'm here," I say. Only half true. I ebb with the tide. I feel the man slipping away from me, but regardless how he sounds or acts, his white blood cell count is rising and his heart is no longer pumping as it should. No matter how ruddy his complexion, his mortal coil is disease ridden. Before long he will be plugged into monitors and IV lines and blood will blacken his urine. He is in agony and he either doesn't know it or he has chosen this way to express it. Where is his true voice? I don't know. I hear only the cry of the sandpipers from the small beach beneath us. *Peet-weet. Peeeet-weeeet.*

Chapter Six

I was never a channel for divine inspiration. I inherited my ideas from other more totally pure minds, but I could visualize my dreams and I was able to project what I saw reflected on the screen of my consciousness. I called it "inner formulation." What is well dreamed, I thought, begins a process of creative preparation. Put differently, a man with inner vision sees the outer world more clearly.

One thing, however, is to soar on the metaphysics of marriage and romance. Another is to wallow in the everyday muck of bad sex, jealousy, addiction, spousal abuse, boredom, infidelity and hellish battles over money. In LA, ninety percent of my clients worked in the film industry, which set the tone and overarching mode for therapy. Obviously, many were aspiring actors. That's a given in any LA office, restaurant, hotel or warehouse. There were also lighting technicians, casting agents, studio execs, assistant editors, location managers and countless industry-related subcontractors. A cinematic superego spreads like source footage over the entire city. A lowly secretary in a catering company that delivers hors d'oeuvres to industry meetings knows more film history than any five people in Missouri. It forced me to become conversant in film lore and jargon so that I could better comprehend my clients who said things like: "I feel like Julia Roberts in 'Pretty Woman' when she tells Richard Gere what's really in her gut." Or "This is like the family court scene in 'A Separation' by Farhadi."

Everything my LA clients verbalized was color-corrected, audio-enhanced and dubbed the night before our session. They directed and starred in their own films. I was the post production chief in charge of turning their performance into a successful marriage, or at least making a trailer to create, market and sell the illusion.

The women I went out with at night were typecast from the women I saw during the day. Talented, gorgeous, ambitious and sexy; in other words, frantic beyond limit. Some played against type or actually played no role at all, but they were rare and usually on their way back to a small town in the Midwest.

I was comfy and well cast in my own film. Leading male in West Hollywood office, earns nice salary, dates starlet types, has fun. My old mentor Harry Higby warned me that I had begun to drift but by then I was too far adrift to listen. Word-of-mouth recommendations, which had always sustained and invigorated my practice, became murmurs, then whispers, then silence. I lost clients and their money as fast as I lost touch with my vision. I no longer participated in online discussions and hits on my web site declined. Finally, the film reached a climactic scene and I bolted like a jail-breaker leaping onto the caboose of a highballing train.

So I was unprepared for an overpriced consultation office on Fisherman's Wharf and Malcolm's cash-stuffed envelope was more welcome than I care to admit. I still suspect I do not fit Monterey's idea of a marriage counselor. Along with a new wardrobe, I need readjustment. Midway through a session with the Garcias on Thursday afternoon, I say, "...like the Vespa scenes in 'Roman Holiday'" and Mr. and Mrs. Garcia look at me as if I am speaking Cantonese. I quickly explain that "Roman Holiday" is a famous romantic comedy with Audrey Hepburn and Gregory Peck. The Garcias tell me they rarely watch TV, "let alone a long movie."

"But I know that Audie guy," Mr. Garcia says. "He was a war hero."

I nod and steer the conversation back onto their relationship. Evidently, LA has taught me that normal people spend all their free time watching films.

When I escort the Garcias out past Reception, Shirley gives me a look and my eye goes to the waiting area, where Beth sits writing in a notebook. I can't say if I am surprised, annoyed or pleased to see her. But I still hear the *peet-weet* of the sandpipers. I warn myself I had better make this encounter short and sweet. She checks her watch and looks up. The gesture gives me pause. Did we arrange to meet? I bid the Garcias goodbye and approach her.

"Should we talk here," she asks, "or walk on the Wharf again?"

Maybe we did make an appointment. Or maybe she has brought another envelope.

"Let's walk," I say.

Once again, the Wharf teems with tourists. The whale boat tours have put up red and yellow banners, advertising group rates and midweek discounts. The aroma of clam chowder, earthy and fishy, wafts on the afternoon breeze. I suggest we avoid the tourists and stroll down the coastal walkway. Still intending to keep our talk short, I'm about to tell her she can't show up at my office any time it strikes her fancy, but I recall she might not be "a well woman" and I can't think of how to put it benignly. Then she says:

"What did you want to see me about?"

"What?"

"Malcolm said you wanted to see me. That I should meet you at 5 o'clock when you finished your session with that couple."

"The Garcias..." I mumble. What's going on here?

Two cyclists force us to step off the path, giving me an instant to rein in my thoughts.

"He said you had something important to tell me," Beth goes on.

"Didn't he tell you himself?"

"Tell me what?"

I stop walking and touch her elbow to stop her as well.

"There's been a misunderstanding," I say. "I'll have to talk to Malcolm first."

Her blue-green eyes betray curiosity tinged by annoyance. "Why all the secrecy? Just tell me whatever it is."

I recall something else Malcolm said—that it will "pierce her like a dagger"—and start walking again. My movement pulls her along.

"I'm not at liberty to," I say.

"You mean like client-therapist privilege?"

"Exactly that."

"But he must think it's okay if he told me to see you."

"The problem is I don't think it's okay."

Although I can't see it, I can sense her rolling her eyes. We pass a family watching a sea otter cavort in the shore ripples. Out on the Bay, two yachts list to starboard, breezing into a fog bank. We come to a bench and sit. Our "short meeting" is in danger of becoming quite long. Beth folds her hands in her lap, a gesture of cultured aplomb. Quiet dazzle, Malcolm said. She motions toward my own hand.

"You're not married," she says. "At least you don't wear a ring."

I raise my hand, wiggle my fingers. "I was married once upon a time. I can't even remember what happened to the ring."

"Isn't that odd for someone in your profession—not to be married?"

"I used to have a friend who was a car mechanic and he didn't own a car." Then I point at her hand and say: "You don't wear a ring either."

"It's in the toilet. Or the ocean. I also don't remember. I had packed my bags and was on my way out the door."

I turn toward her. Neither she nor Malcolm gave me this version of the story. "What stopped you?"

"Malcolm. He pleaded with me to see you."

I can't imagine him pleading with anyone for anything. I should end the conversation here or spin it in a new direction, but the best I can do is hesitate. "So... you still thought there was hope of saving your marriage?"

"Not at all. I had been urging him to get professional help since the day we married. It was a chance to finally get him some. A kind of parting gift." She pauses, looks at the fog bank where the two yachts have vanished. "Then along came the cancer."

"You stuck around because of his illness?"

"Who would leave? Two months... two years later, you still have to live with yourself."

A minute ago I was yammering about client-therapist privilege; now I'm trespassing all over restricted turf. "But you describe it like you've already left him... in thought if not in deed."

She looks at me curiously, as if I've just materialized on the bench next to her. "I don't need a priest to tell me I'm married," she says, "or a judge to tell me I'm separated."

Holding her gaze, I observe a kind of savage sincerity; she defends herself from her own doubts as well as the world's judgment.

"Marriage wasn't what you imagined it would be," I say.

"That's putting it nicely. I thought I was getting day and I got night." She glances again at the sea, turns back to me. "Do women ever ask you what men look for in them?"

"Are you asking?"

She smiles slightly. "I suppose I am."

"Then I think you're asking a question you already know the answer to."

"Hmm," she replies cryptically. "You're sardonic today. It's not like you."

She has caught me. Caught me throwing up a nervous barrier right after learning she is—at least in her own mind—single and free. What happened to my plan to keep this short? I become aware of the sea lions and harbor seals. Have they been moaning all this time? I haven't heard a thing. But now I hear a prolonged buzzing. Beth reaches into her purse and turns off the alarm on her cell phone. She takes out a small pill canister and bottle of water.

"Sorry," she says, "but if I don't do it now I'll forget." She washes down a pill with a sip of water. "I get cluster headaches and I've been microdosing with psilocybin. It's the only thing I've found that works."

"A few of my clients use it for anxiety and depression."

"That too. It cheers me up." She smiles as if she has cheered up on the spot. "But I won't let you off the hook. What do you think men look for in women?"

"They're looking for God."

She lets out a delightful burst of laughter. "I think the same. Let me ask you something else. Do you know *The Coast Quarterly?*"

I shake my head.

"It's a literary-art journal. They sell it in Monterey, Carmel and Santa Cruz bookstores."

"I don't think I've heard of it."

"Nobody else has either, but it's been around for a half dozen years. It doesn't prosper, but it survives. It's partially funded by a foundation."

She tells me that she is the journal's senior editor and that most issues contain a selection of poems, short stories, critical essays and the occasional book review. An illustrated six-page section, often with a tipped-in color plate, appears in the center of the quarterly and coincides with some artist's opening in San Francisco or LA.

"We also do interviews," she says, "and I wonder if you'd be interested."

"In subscribing?"

"In being interviewed. We try to do one themed issue a year. We've dedicated issues to 'Birth and Beauty,' 'Design,' 'War and Revolution' and 'Enlightenment.' I considered doing an issue on "Death and Dying" for obvious personal reasons, but every quarterly on the planet has already drummed the topic into dust. So I thought, why not marriage?"

I can't stop from squeezing my hands together. Now I'm certain this has gone on too long. I don't know this woman, I think. More to the point, she doesn't know me. She knows a dead and gone version of me, an extinct YouTube creature on a blurry screen. I feel a chill penetrate my backbone.

"But... I'm not famous or well known."

"Neither is *The Coast Quarterly*. For that matter, neither are our contributors. Occasionally, we coerce some prize winner to grace us with a piece, but most of our manuscripts come in over the transom."

Her blue-green eyes regard me quizzically before she goes on: "I thought we might do a three-part piece similar to your workshop at Esalen. For the quarterly and as a podcast." Editorial enthusiasm mounting, she adds: "Now that I think of it, I might request the rights for Corso's poem *Marriage*."

I restrain myself from pronouncing the word *Who?* She delays a moment longer and finally says, "Well, I don't need an answer right this minute, so give it some thought."

The fog has crept in off the horizon and spread over the Wharf. On our way back down the path, Beth points out a spray of sunlight beyond the moored boats. I should walk her to wherever she has parked her car, but I come to a stop near the Counseling Center, fighting down the urge to drag out more time with her. She slings her purse over her opposite shoulder, makes ready to leave.

"You still don't want to tell me the big secret?" she says.

I hesitate. I feel like we've been together for hours and the interview has already begun.

"I have to talk to Malcolm first." I reply.

Chapter Seven

I have been poring over manuals on death and dying but now I dig into unpacked cardboard boxes and unearth ancient volumes. I bury myself in the texts of my defunct self. I read voraciously. I read until my eyes sting. Imago Relationship Therapy, Gottman's "The Seven Principles for Making Marriage Work," Jung, Rilke, John of the Cross, Orpheus and Eurydice, twin soul, twin flame.

Around my new living room, books gape open like feathers plucked and scattered in all directions. I am trying to feed my mind but I feel like I am feeding chickens and must protect them from hawks. The contrast between the ideal and the real. I can't deny it. Beth's suggestion of an interview is an invitation to see again. Exactly what I said I wanted. Yet now I tremble.

I return to the used bookstore on Lighthouse Avenue and poke through their extensive section on Metaphysics. Scanning texts, I find I have something in common with Spinoza, Thomas Aquinas, Kant, Kierkegaard and Nietzsche. They all remained unmarried. In "Either/Or: A Fragment of Life," Kierkegaard wrote: "If you marry, you will regret it; if you do not marry, you will also regret it." Plato thought that anyone who "disobeyed the duty to marry" should pay a yearly fine.

I purchase a copy of "The Love Letters of Abelard

and Heloise" at the counter where I spot a few copies of *The Coast Quarterly*. The clerk tells me they have been on display for over a month, so I failed to notice them on my last visit.

"It's the most recent issue," he says. "Good stuff."

I buy one and open to the masthead. The founder and senior editor is Elizabeth Dijkstra. There is a fiction editor, a poetry editor, an art editor, a publishing manager, two interns and four manuscript readers. Credit is given to the Dijkstra Foundation for "generous support."

I unchain my bike and pedal back home, where I google Elizabeth Dijkstra and find a photograph of a younger Beth, still a dishwater blond but with longer disheveled hair. Biographical data shows that she attended Yale, where she majored in French literature and, as a junior, became an assistant editor on the Yale Review. She spent her senior year in Paris at the Sorbonne, and worked at *Bleu Nuit,* a dual language literary journal. Upon her return to the States, she lived in Brooklyn for two years, in New Haven for one and then Den Hague for two more, employed in an unspecified capacity by the Dijkstra Foundation, started by her great grandfather, Lukas Kees Dijkstra, a Dutch entrepreneur and investment banker. A master's degree back at the Sorbonne came later, then a "sabbatical." Some years her whereabouts and doings are unexplained. When the Dijkstra Foundation established an office in San Francisco, she moved to California. One year later she founded and published the first issue of *The Coast Quarterly*. The biography makes no mention of marriage.

I page through *The Coast Quarterly* and find poems and essays devoted to war and revolution, then an interview with a former Navy Seal turned Christian pacifist. The interviewer is Beth. Some of her questions strike me as unnecessarily contentious, verging on aggression. Or maybe I'm just back pedaling from a return journey to Esalen. It doesn't matter. Where I must now return is to death and dying, but I google Malcolm Favor and find no mention of the man. I tell myself it doesn't matter either. What matters is that I have taken on a dire responsibility and need to address it.

First step is to get my thoughts in order. I pack up all the books scattered around the living room and stuff them along with Abelard and Heloise back into the cardboard moving boxes. Then I remount my bike and pedal down to the Wharf. The air is redolent of sea food and cotton candy. I glide onto the bike path. The barking of the sea lions seems loud today. Another cyclist pedals in front of me, a small child bouncing in a baby seat. The child slurps at an ice cream cone and a bounce leaves a vanilla smudge on a pug nose. I pass a glass-bottom boat floating across harbor waters. I squeeze the brakes and roll to a stop. A half dozen tourists sit in the boat, peering down at underwater flora and fauna. I must do the same, I think. Tomorrow at Pacific House I have to peer into Malcolm's depths, not into Google. I'm charged with helping the man, but before I can do that, I have to clear my own muddy water.

A wooden deck chair and fold-out table stand beside the flat granite boulder at the cliff edge. Malcolm sits in the chair, breaking a chunk off a loaf of French bread. He is unshaven and depleted, but still appears regal against the backdrop of orange sky and turbulent sea, a silver-haired king at the border of his realm. His scepter—the eagle's beak cane—rests at his side. I wonder if this is what attracted Beth, a monarch presence, the illusion of an eternal father-figure king.

"My diet has recently undergone a change," he says, offering me the loaf. "Would you care for some of my meager repast?"

I accept the bread, step around the table and sit on the granite boulder. The view to to the south is of dark mountains jutting into the sea.

"It's the Santa Lucia Range, isn't it?" I ask, tearing at the bread.

"Still standing."

Shifting his weight in the chair, he suppresses a grunt of pain. I bite into the bread and chew as if concentrated on the taste, giving him a moment to find a new position. A single gull circles above us, cawing, its sharp eye on the bread. Like a hawk, I think.

"Let's begin our session today with a story," Malcolm says.

I set the loaf onto the table within his reach. Time to clear the water. "First I want to know if you've told Beth yet."

"We agreed you would tell her."

"We both know we agreed to no such thing."

"Well, she isn't here today. By the way, how did you get in?"

"Yetta."

"Ah, the loyal Yetta." He reaches for the bread, suppressing another grunt. "So I've been thinking about death," he says, "and releasing trauma. I know a little about trauma. You see, I grew up in rural Pennsylvania. My mother was a housewife and my father a carpenter of sorts." Reading my thoughts, he shakes his silver head. "No, I do not come from money. I come from thwarted dreams. My father hoped I might become a carpenter too. In a way, I did. That's what an architect is—the 'head carpenter'."

"You're an architect?"

"That's what I just said."

Long ago I learned to set aside what a client is saying and put my attention on why and how they are saying it. Now I have a fleeting impression of an off-key note and wonder if Malcolm is making this up, the way someone makes up a dream; the truth is still there, but hidden beneath a veil of false sleep.

"My father was a hunter," he goes on. "Every deer season he marched out into the Pennsylvania woods with a gang of his friends, drinking rotgut whiskey by the gallon, tripping over high-powered rifles. One time my uncle shot off half his foot. The other men considered it bad luck, part of the dangers hunters face when tracking game."

At twelve years old, Malcolm says, he was forced to join the outings. His father and the other men demanded that he swig gulps of the murderous whiskey. Head spinning, he stumbled down forest paths. Then he and his father waited in a blind. Soon Malcolm's chance came and by some outlandish stroke of beginner's luck he brought down a seven-point stag with a single shot.

The men gutted the deer with buck knives as Malcolm watched hot bowels splash and steam on the forest floor. Then the men grabbed him, pinning his arms. They draped the disemboweled deer carcass over his head and tied him to a tree. They laughed, chanted some ancient hunting song and stumbled back to their cabin to drink more whiskey.

All the hunters had undergone a similar initiation ritual, Malcolm tells me. Traditionally, it lasted a half hour. But some of them passed out and others left for home while afternoon turned to evening and then night. In the forest Malcolm stood lashed to the tree, the deer cowl over his head, the stench of drying blood and animal flesh burning his nostrils. As the night passed, he stared into darkness at exactly the point, he imagined, where the dead creature's eyes were placed over his own. In the morning his father arrived home and his mother said *Where's the boy?* An hour later Malcolm's first hunting excursion ended.

"So what do you think of that?" he asks.

"I think it sounds horrendous," I murmur. "And traumatic." Also extreme; again I wonder how much of it is true.

He flashes a weak smile. "I knew it was a story you would enjoy."

Something is wrong here. I can't perceive the *why* behind the telling of the tale. He breaks off another piece of bread and tosses it over the side of the cliff. The gull swoops downward. The ocean emits a roar.

"Did you try to escape?" I ask.

The question catches him off guard. The first time I have seen him lose his regal air.

"Escape what?" he says.

"Your situation. You were a child hunter converted into the hunted. It must have been terrifying. Did you try to get away?"

"I just told you. A pack of drunken men lashed me to a tree."

"Yes, but did you try to wiggle free or tear at the ropes with your fingers? Did you shout for help? You were there all night. Think back. What were your hands doing?"

"I have told you this story," he says angrily, "because I want to escape the past before I die. Will you help me or not, Mr. Therapist?"

The more aggression in his voice, the louder he cries for help, lashed to a tree or not. I am here to untie the knots, to release him.

"I think there is more to your story..." I say slowly, pronouncing the word *story* with a note of skepticism. "Something more you want to tell me."

"Correct," he says, regaining his composure. "You remember I spoke to you about deer, their eating habits. Well, they often come here at night." He gestures at the field. "They are led by the Ghost Deer."

I cock my head to the side. "A ghost?"

"Correct again."

"Malcolm, it sounds to me like you might be talking about a ghost from your past."

"If so, many other people must share my past. Ask around. The Ghost Deer is a large albino stag. It roams Del Monte Forest." He looks directly at me. "On two separate occasions I have faced the creature here in this yard at night. His many pointed antlers gleam and his primordial eyes shine. I have looked straight into those eyes." He pauses, screws his tired eyes into mine. "So what do you think now?" he demands.

I wanted to clear turbid water and peer into his depths but the water has just clouded even more. I am trying to see and this man blinds me, covers me in shadow. I rise off the granite boulder.

"The same thing I thought before. That you need to tell Beth about your heart condition. I'm not going to continue these sessions until you do."

"You have to continue," he says. "You gave your word."

I step away from the boulder. "I'll ask Yetta to show me out."

Chapter Eight

A blazing fireplace in a deserted home. No one around except the hostess, a child psychologist, who throws a little bash every autumn for the Counseling Center therapists and their partners. I didn't want to attend her party and now I have mistakenly arrived a half hour early. Taken by surprise, she refuses my offer of help and parks me with a beer in front of the fireplace. As she runs off into the kitchen, I stare at the flames in an empty room I expected to be packed and noisy.

It gives me a quiet moment alone, nothing to do except sip beer. Like it or not, I need the break. Taking on Malcolm and *The Coast Quarterly* interview at the same time may not have been a wise idea. They coexist badly. Too much to think about and not enough time to do the thinking. The flames throw heat onto my face as an ormulo-mounted clock ticks on the mantle above me.

Until now, I have only met a few of the therapists at the Center, a quick *hello* in the hallway, a smile or nod in passing. In a few minutes I will have to engage in party talk, describe myself, explain my existence, chat about LA, offer reasons for my move, field questions with a grin and good grace. Is it a big change for you? Are you glad to get out of LA or do you miss the excitement? Why don't you wear a sweater and jeans like everyone else?

The hostess now dressed in a barbecue apron scurries out of the kitchen bearing a tray of seafood canapés. Her eyes widen as if seeing me for the first time. Then she remembers, smiles and says: "Don't let the fire die out!"

Good therapeutical advice. I pick up a compressed wood log and drop it onto the flames. The fire crackles and pops and my wayward consciousness is warmed and welcomed back to center.

The other guests show up on time. To my amusement, they bring along kids and dogs, including the largest, ugliest bulldog I have ever seen. Frederick Kline arrives, the goody-two-shoes president of the Monterey Counseling Center. He introduces unknown people to me. They give my hand a firm shake. Australian, Chinese, Sicilian, black/white American, a little of everything.

Low-key rock music merges into laughter and more greetings. A pretty social worker named Jenny asks how I am getting on at the Center, describes the location of her office, offers help if I need any. The kids race around the backyard like frenzied chimpanzees, then come back inside and behave themselves. Nobody has to warn them. I try to imagine an LA party with dogs, kids and no coke and finally realize I need to shed my ill humor. Nobody here is whacked out on drugs or imagined fame. I am in the presence of twenty friendly, warm-hearted people rather than two dozen egos bouncing off the walls. We eat and drink and talk about school problems, the baseball playoffs, the recent lunge feeding, a new proposal at the Aquarium, a multiple traffic accident near Seaside. Every so often I toss another log onto the fire; it has become my duty. "Thanks, Ryan!" the hostess calls from across the room.

People shove furniture aside, turn up the music and begin to dance. Dogs bark and kids hip-hop around the periphery. Jenny the social worker drags me out onto the floor. I resist and am awkward but her bubbly spirit overwhelms my LA cool and we rock and roll until we are both laughing and covered in sweat. When did I last have such fun? We collapse onto a sofa and reach for more beer. Others do likewise and soon the music dies down. I sip beer and smile at the air, at the ceiling. I have picked the right soil, I think, now I need to replant myself. And somehow help a dying man transmute anger into acceptance.

Near my feet, a few of the kids poke and pull at the enormous bulldog's wrinkled mug, his hideous ears. The dog pants heavily but shows no irritation. Ugly all right, but full of patience. I reach down and scratch his ample belly.

"What's his name?" I ask the kids.

"His name is Mr. Gus," a young boy answers, "but we call him Gus for short. Do you have a dog, sir?"

Sir? Who has raised these kids and in what universe do they exist?

"Not now," I answer, "but when I was your age my family had a terrier named Muffy."

The boy looks at me doubtfully. "That isn't a real dog's name."

"You're right," I say. "Normally it isn't, but Muffy wasn't normal so that was her name."

"Oh." He thinks for a moment. "Did Muffy bark?"

"Only when a ghost was in the house."

The other kids stop poking at Mr. Gus and look up at me. Enlarged eyes and prodigious silence. A little girl with a pony tail says, "You had ghosts in your house?"

"Seven of them. Most were friendly but two could be grumpy. They had a pet too, a ghost deer."

"No way!" the boy says. "A deer can't be a ghost!"

I have forgotten Jenny who is still sitting beside me. "Have you seen it?" she asks.

I turn toward her. "You mean it's real?"

A sheen of sweat still gleams on her pretty face. "It's part of local lore," she says, "an occasional subject for the newspapers and guidebooks. I've seen it a couple of times over the years. Always in Del Monte Forest. I go jogging there. When one deer appears, two or three others usually follow, but it always seems to be alone. Strange-looking creature."

The kids become bored with what has turned into an adult conversation. They go back to poking at Mr. Gus.

"Did you see its eyes?" I ask.

She thinks back. "Actually, now that you say, I guess I did." She tells me the last time was about two years ago, just before evening. "The fog was in. Kind of misty, like how it gets in the woods. I pulled up to catch my breath and gulp some water and there it was, about thirty yards away, watching me through the trees." A shiver passes over her. "I guess it was kind of spooky."

"Sounds like it," I say.

Sounds like it because now I feel spooked as well. I rise off the sofa, pick up another compressed log and drop it onto the fire.

Spyglass Woods Drive runs through some dense foliage in Del Monte Forest and then past a few isolated houses. I turn onto a gravel path, pedal along for a while, lose my way in the trees and somehow come out on the coast at Seal Rock Creek Beach, small and sandy, at the mouth of Seal Rock Creek. I dismount and push the bike across the parking lot to a pay telescope, where I wait in a line of tourists. The man behind me turns out to be a local from Carmel, who tells me that during the summer months the fog can get so thick you can't see out to Seal Rock. We chat about the fog and bird life and then my turn at the telescope comes. I get a close-up view of barking sea lions and harbor seals and scores of fluttering gulls.

I push my bike around the area. Down on the beach, sandpipers skitter after the waves. Everywhere danger signs warn tourists not to climb onto the rocks to take selfies. Someone has scribbled a personal note on one of the signs: "I saw a monster wave drag a boy out to sea. Please don't join him."

I run into the Carmel man again and learn he is not so local. He moved here from North Dakota a dozen years ago and still misses the snow. "I moved to get away from the stuff," he says, "and now it's the only thing I miss."

When I leave him, I reflect on my own move from LA. Do I miss anything? Not snow, that's for sure. I think a moment longer and have to admit I miss my breezy, hang-loose lifestyle. A life minus the burden of bringing peace of mind to a dying client.

Malcolm sits at the table near the cliff edge, cloudy gray sky behind him, large waves rolling in. A surge of determination quickens my steps over the last few yards to the granite boulder. As I take my seat, heat rises out of my solar plexus. Malcolm sits hunched forward, leaning onto the tabletop for support. He looks weak, possibly in pain. He wears dark sunglasses and a three-day growth of gray whiskers. His mouth hangs open. Not the same man I saw a few days ago.

"My eyes have become light sensitive," he says, gesturing at his sunglasses, "but I see you still haven't told my wife."

"I told you I wasn't going to."

"In a way, it's good that you haven't." He raps the eagle's beak cane against the table edge. "Better bad news in one hard sledgehammer hit than the tap tap tap of repeated blows."

I can no longer see his eyes but I sense that behind the dark glasses they are hyper-vigilant. "What do you mean?"

The wind blows in from the west, impelling the five-foot breakers toward shore. Wave faces like steel walls rush toward us. Malcolm gives the cane a last rap against the table.

"I mean I have received the final downgrade. The medical team assembled en masse—oncologist, cardiologist, their little helpers—to issue the news. Ganging up on me so I couldn't argue, I suppose."

My voice tightens. "What did they say?"

"That my cancer is raging like a forest fire and my heart is a bomb about to explode. They claim there is no longer anything they can do. They do not even wish to see me again."

"They said it like that?"

"They said it is time for morphine, priests and hospice care, even though the cardiologist is squeamish about the morphine. You must tell my wife."

This is his own sledgehammer blow of reprisal, I think. He projects his anger at the doctors and at life onto me. He will not stop until he forces me to do his bidding, forces me to admit there is no peace of mind left for him. I fear he might rise from his chair and throw himself off the cliff edge. Not out of desperation, but out of venom and gall. The chill of the granite boulder rises into me.

"You already have my answer on that," I reply.

"Very well. One day soon I will die and that is how my wife will find out. Imagine when she comes upon a note explaining how I begged you to help me tell her and how you refused... refused a dying man's last request."

He knows exactly where and how to push my buttons. "Listen, Malcolm, I'm here to help you find some tranquility, not to play games. What're you trying to pull?"

"Your strings," he answers calmly. "What did you think—that you would come out here, admire the view, collect a wad of cash, and that *you* would control the conversation? You might as well try to control these waves, stop them from coming in so fast."

It's not just anger, but a desire to make me feel inadequate and unnecessary. He exudes a kind of gluttony for perverse triumph. Am I wanted here? Or am I just out of my depth as much as he implies, afraid to tell Beth because I know he's right, that the news will be a dagger thrust?

"I am what you would describe as *wealthy,*" he goes on, wincing again. "I have made a lot of money in my life. But my wife comes from real money, wealth the likes of which you can't imagine. It gives her a European bank-vault view of the world. She believes the way to solve any problem is by contracting laborers and putting them to work. Any wrinkle in the fabric of life and she hires a peasant to iron it out. She has hired you as an existential babysitter to nurse me toward some New Age inner calm. But she is beginning to doubt you are addressing the problem she has hired you to solve. This is the real reason she wants to interview you for her artsy journal. To find out if you are who she erroneously thinks you are."

This catches me unawares. I somehow assumed Beth rarely speaks to him now and that he wouldn't know about the interview.

"It seems you help foster her doubts," I say.

"She doesn't need help for that. Her troubled mind feeds on doubt like a cow munching on grass. She grazes on fear. She invents tales that explain she is a penniless princess living in a palace possessed by her royal family but never by her. She owns nothing but the clothes she wears, the poetry she prints. Lies and more lies. Her confused misgivings have led her into nervous crackups. Ask her if you *doubt* me."

Never in my professional life have I argued back and forth, trading glib and sarcastic remarks with a client about his wife. I must quell the sensation that I am getting nowhere, that, as I suspected from the start, I am causing more harm than good. But this last revelation has taken me by surprise.

"Pacific House belongs to Beth?" I say.

"Of course it does. She only pretends otherwise. My wife is strung out on drugs and bookish fantasy."

I am sick of hearing him say the words *my wife*. Not once has he called her by name. As before, I can't imagine what unearthly power ever brought the two of them together. They aren't even opposites who might attract. They are antipodal, dissonant, retrograde.

"We had very little time before," I say firmly. "You've just told me we now have even less. We have to stop wasting it."

"And how will we do that?"

"By taking a hard look at reality."

"You take it," he says, wincing again as he turns toward the waves. "And tell me what you see."

"I see the cancer isn't what's killing you," I say. "You come out here for fresh air because you're suffocating."

He remains quiet, as if contemplating my words. "Sometimes I have the impression," he says, "that you are one of these soft, caring souls who has a desperate need to save other souls only because you can't save your own."

I am sliding backwards. My own peace of mind—the little I have—is reverse somersaulting downhill. I wonder if he has even the vaguest desire to heal. Is his cynicism normal for the terminal phase or is it a reckless yearning for oblivion?

He raps the eagle's beak cane against the table again and speaks abruptly. "That ends our session for today. I am tired of discussing life's values."

Chapter Nine

The stories, poems, essays and artwork featured in our special marriage-themed issue of The Coast Quarterly *are enlivened by this three-part interview with MFT-licensed therapist Ryan Mathiesson. A recent arrival to the Monterey Peninsula, Ryan Mathiesson brings with him twenty years of experience counseling troubled couples in both San Diego and Los Angeles. His long and extensive studies on wedlock include Imago Relationship Therapy, the Gottman Method and EFT. He has been a frequent contributor to popular internet forums and discussion groups and his highly acclaimed Esalen workshop,* The Marriage Dance, *may be viewed on YouTube.*

Founding Editor Elizabeth Dijkstra met Ryan Mathiesson in our Carmel office on—what else?—a foggy day, and together they tried to dispel some of the mist floating around this ancient courtship ritual. So without further dew, we present an at-times unholy trinity of interviews entitled: The Basics, The Metaphysics, *and* The Marriage Dance. *As always, the podcast of this exchange is freely available to subscribers on* The Coast Quarterly *webpage.*

ED: Before jumping into the metaphysics and poetry of marriage, I thought we might first look at some of the down-to-earth basics.

RM: You mean sex?

ED: (laughs) Okay, let's start there. What can you tell us?

RM: In our very recent history as a society, we have gone from having sexual relations for purely reproductive reasons to screwing our brains out for purely personal pleasure.

ED: You're against personal pleasure?

RM: Hardly. I'm all for it. Up to a point.

ED: And that point is?

RM: Different for everyone. But it involves some kind of limit or boundary, whether imposed by an individual, a religion or a culture. Without it we enter uncharted territory "where there be dragons." Inevitably, we fall off the map or get eaten alive by sea monsters.

ED: You're speaking of separation and divorce, of affairs and infidelity?

RM: When we lose our way we need to return to our origins. Especially when we're engaged in a confused search for new values in a chaotic society.

ED: Haven't unfaithful spouses and affairs existed since the beginning of time?

RM: But never before with society's raging approval, never before with genital imagery dripping off every magazine cover at the corner newsstand, never with billboards, films, television and internet sites injecting a daily dose of erotica into our dazed and disturbed minds. Eight-year-old children who used to frolic in the fresh air with the family bulldog now have duck-soup access to porn sites displaying humans having sex with animals. We can't even comprehend the ramifications, the psychic damage.

ED: So tell us about divorce in a world of dazed minds.

RM: Despite the overwhelming dangers of divorce, about nine out of every ten people still opt for marriage. When the first marriage fails, three out of four divorcees choose to marry again, even though a second marriage increases the risk for divorce. No one has yet figured it out, but for some reason third marriages have a slightly better success rate. *(pauses)* In my experience, many husbands and wives do not even know why their spouses file for divorce. Also, I don't want to make light of this. Not every couple in therapy is there because of carefree infidelity. Many suffer terrible afflictions.

ED: Such as?

RM: The death of a child, PTSD, psychosis, addiction, attempted suicide.

ED: What about the LGBTQ community? Do you counsel many couples who are transgender, lesbian, gay...?

RM: Rarely. Sometimes I find myself talking to a person who has come out of the closet in the middle of a marriage but, by and large, the LGBTQ community doesn't come to me for counseling.

ED: Why not?

RM: You would have to ask them, but as far as I'm

able to understand, they prefer to seek counseling from an LGBTQ therapist, someone who perhaps better relates to their circumstances and needs.

ED: Then you wouldn't refuse to counsel a transgender couple?

RM: Of course not. I treat human beings. Especially if I think I can help.

ED: Are there couples who you can't help?

RM: Sometimes marriage isn't the problem for a couple. One or both of the individuals may have a serious mental health issue. They don't need a marriage therapist. They need a psychiatrist.

ED: How do you recognize these individuals?

RM: There may be aggressive language or violent behavior.

ED: Returning to divorce. Are we any better off divorced than we were married?

RM: You can find statistics on anything you want but, referring once again to the basics, I'd say we don't do well. Not well at all. Naturally, many people end up happier afterwards but divorce usually tears our heart out even when we're the ones who instigate it for our betterment. We have solemnly sworn to be with another person for the rest of our lives and now we are running for the hills. Divorce triggers depression, anxiety, trauma, rage and hopelessness. It would seem we're designed to be together.

ED: No matter the hell it puts us through?

RM: If it didn't put us though hell, I guess I wouldn't have work.

ED: Nuns and monks spend their lives alone.

RM: Not exactly. They marry Jesus. At least that's what John of the Cross said. Christ is the bridegroom; our soul is the bride. Though that might be a different kind of hell. Or heaven.

ED: Then let's get back to sex. How often is it the reason marriages go bad?

RM: Studies on separation and divorce always list infidelity as one of the prime causes but there are many others: lack of commitment, arguments, financial problems, religious differences, getting married too young, substance abuse. It's a long list, often topped off by a final straw.

ED: Every case must be different but if you could speak generally for a moment... Is there any basic therapy you use with troubled couples?

RM: I try to guide them back to their origins. It is not only society that needs to go there. We have a longing to reground ourselves in the great achievements of the past, to re-identify with an archetypal essence of being. What does that mean? In the case of a troubled couple, it can mean that the sacred vows and resplendent moments in their shared past become an inspiration for a new beginning. The seed of a new day depends upon the seed of yesteryear. A process of transfiguration.

ED: Would some type of premarital relationship training help at the start?

RM: It would help a lot, but we're already too busy choosing dreamy music for our celestial wedding ceremony. We're thinking about wearing pretty clothes and having someone take stunning photographs to enshrine our moment of happiness. Our concepts are so tightly tangled it's almost impossible to unravel them. We all have friends whose idyllic wedding we attended and whose idyllic relationship we admired over the years. Often they tell us they are not only in love, they are each other's best friends. Then one day a vulgar, violent separation occurs. The knives come out and we see that their idyllic rapport had nothing to do with friendship. They simply rooted for the same baseball team or liked the same ice cream, the same music and movies. They mistook that for friendship.

ED: Much of what you have told us so far has a cynical ring. Are you pessimistic about marriage?

RM: I believe in romance, tenderness and courtship. I also believe in holding hands and making love, in passion, enchantment, infatuation and flirtation, which is a lost art. I even believe in Valentine's Day. But I also believe in facing reality.

ED: And how do we do that?

RM: With courage, caution and concentration. Also you can try something else, but once again, it takes courage.

ED: Tell us. We'll be brave.

RM: Face your lover. Sit down in front of him or

her, look directly into his or her eyes and say, "I love you." Yes, I know it sounds trite, but try not to say it in a singsong or baby voice, as if you were playing around or mocking yourself for being so corny. Say it with conviction and seriousness. Speak from the silent center of your heart. You will feel some small thing inside you break. It doesn't matter if you say it once a year or once every day. It takes guts to do it and if you declare your love truthfully and sincerely, that small thing will break and you will feel it. Then ask yourself when was the last time your lover looked deep into your eyes and told you. Really told you so that it sent a vibrant thrill into you and awakened your entire being, filling you with excitement and profound gratitude. If that hasn't happened for a while, you need to make it happen, demand that it happen. But it always takes courage.

ED: And going to the personal, have you declared your love to anyone recently?

RM: (hesitates) Not for a while.

ED: Why not?

RM: It isn't something you do offhandedly. You need to truly feel it and, of course, you need a worthy recipient.

ED: Is it possible that your very profession and line of work prevent you from finding a worthy recipient?

RM: I'm not following you...

ED: Every day of the week you witness the vulgarity and violence you just described. Squabbling couples and horrifying scenes. Does it affect you personally, make you reluctant or wary of getting into the ring—wearing the ring—of married life yourself?

RM: I'd like to think that I'm not as pessimistic as your questions are beginning to suggest. I said I believed in facing reality, but I also said that I'm all for tenderness, romance, enchantment—

ED: Yes, but you didn't include marriage in that list. Do you believe in marriage?

RM: It's like asking a priest if he believes in religion.

ED: Is that how you think of yourself when you're counseling distraught couples—as a priest?

RM: I didn't say that. Nor would I.

ED: Nonetheless, in many religions, marriage is a sacrament performed by a priest. Even if you don't believe in marriage for yourself personally, do you see it as a sacred act?

RM: I also didn't say that I don't believe in it personally.

ED: It was implied.

RM: Not by me.

ED: What about marriage as a sacred act?

RM: I don't understand where we're going here...

ED: Then let me be more precise. You are a marriage therapist who is unmarried. Speaking solely in terms of the personal, are you yourself open to marriage?

RM: I'm no different from anyone else. We all seek a twin soul.

ED: That sounds like a perfect transition into Part 2 of our interview, *The Metaphysics of Marriage.* So let's stop here for now, catch our collective breath and come back to it. See you then.

CHAPTER TEN

"I don't know what got into me," Beth says. "My god, I felt like I was attacking you."

"Then we both felt the same thing," I reply hotly. But my anger disguises mounting relief, relief that the interview is over and I'm still in one piece.

"Are—are you all right?" she asks.

"Feeling a bit raw..." My muttered tone fashions more anger. "...but I'll survive."

She glances at Bernie, a twenty-year-old intern, who busies himself packing the microphones and their shields back in their boxes. He winds up wires and plugs, glancing everywhere in the small office except at Beth and me. I sense him trying to become invisible.

Beth summons an authoritative voice. "Thanks, Bernie. You've been great. We'll take it from here."

Bernie forces a smile, snatches up his things, scurries out the door. Neither Beth nor I move. Late afternoon ocean light sprays through fog and then through the windows into the room. There are ceiling-high shelves stuffed with literary journals and chapbooks, two wooden desks, a vintage sofa and matching armchair. The place emanates old world flair. At the rear there is a bathroom with a shower and a kitchenette where a mini-fridge gurgles. All of this within one of Carmel's fairy-tale cottages, a place that appears from the outside as though it holds only whimsical and idyllic events. I hear waves crashing onto the nearby beach or maybe I imagine the sound. I didn't hear it during the interview.

"We were going so good," Beth says, "until I... took that detour. I'm so sorry. But I'll listen to it and edit out any—"

"Leave it," I say. "It is what it was. For good or not so good."

She studies me, looks down at her hands. I should leave but I can't bring myself to rise to my feet. My joints ache, my bones are tired. I feel like I've just passed through narrow rapids struggling for calm waters. The control and poise needed to reach a steady state of inner stability. Wobbling, I finally rise to my feet. The sunlight in the room is heavy now; dust motes glitter and dance near the windows.

"At least let me buy you a drink," Beth says. "You deserve one."

"I deserve two," I reply.

She gives a laugh. "Okay, two. We can go to Paddy's. It's just down Ocean Ave."

She locks up and we walk off. The misty air is damp and bracing, the sound of waves now real. We turn onto Ocean Ave.

"I'm usually a wine person," she says.

"I can go with that."

I'm too tired to go any other way, but our short exchange suggests that something stronger is called for.

When we come to Paddy's Pub, it is packed and loud. We stand on the street, looking at the windows. Large wall-mounted screens show a 49ers game in progress. Patrons shout encouragement at the screens.

"Listen," Beth says. "MaryAnn, our fiction editor, keeps a bottle of something in the fridge. Something Polish, I think. She wouldn't mind."

"Sounds perfect," I say, still going along.

We walk back the way we have come. In the short time we have been gone, the fog has grown thicker, vanquishing the last rays of ocean light, engulfing the fairy-tale cottage. Dust motes no longer dance inside the office. Beth finds a bottle of slivovitz in the freezer and brings it to the sofa. She says some Polish poet whose name she can't pronounce recommends drinking it chilled but without ice. She pours two measures into cocktail glasses. We sit on the vintage sofa and clink glasses but make no toast. I take a sip and the chilled liquor runs hot across my palate. I no longer hear or imagine I hear waves crashing onto the beach. I can't recall a single word I said during the interview. Did I sound noble? Or did I sound like I was repeating everything I read over the last week? I should get on my way. Why do I always feel I need to cut short my time with this woman? Her blue-green gaze is slightly moist. She says:

"Do you think I was taking out my failed marriage on you... projecting dirt I'd like to throw at Malcolm?"

I shrug. "I don't know. Maybe."

"Well, that's not good."

I don't want the conversation to go in Malcolm's direction, so I return to my feeling of relief, raise my glass to the room, try to change the subject. "It's nice in here. Charming and cozy and... literary, for lack of a better word."

"It's wonderful," she replies intensely. "Much better than that big ugly house."

"Pacific House is big," I agree, "but not many people would call it ugly."

She frowns. "They see a piece of prime real estate. They don't live inside with the ugliness." She pats the sofa cushion between us. "One of the reasons I spend my nights here."

I regard her quizzically but she looks away, sips slivovitz.

"Is this office part of your foundation?" I ask.

"It's part of the Dijkstra Foundation," she answers, "which, besides the surname and some nice perks, has very little to do with me."

"I thought—"

"It's what most people think. It's certainly what Malcolm thought."

She waits for a reaction I do not give, then goes on to tell me about her great grandfather and the Foundation, which she says was established for "wise investments in art, humanitarian aid, land development and institutions designed to edify and educate humanity." Verbatim the article I read online. I ask if *The Coast Quarterly* qualified as "edifying humanity."

"After a year of merciless scrutiny," she replies. "To rule out any hint of nepotism."

She adds that all direct descendants in the Dijkstra lineage are entitled to free rent, usually in the form of a luxury urban dwelling or country estate. A monthly stipend to cover frugal living expenses is included. But nothing else. There is no inheritance or endowment. She does not and may not own any Foundation dwelling, or any furnishing, artwork or accessory therein contained. The same rules apply to her two brothers and to various cousins she has never met. Her great grandfather was generous but believed in old-fashioned virtues like self-reliance, restraint and thrift. If she wants new shoes, she must pay for them out of her monthly stipend or earn the money elsewhere.

She tells me all this as if in defense of an accusation. I nod with interest, but my thoughts leap to Malcolm's blast—*Penniless princess. Lies and more lies.* When she shifts positions on the sofa, I take a quick look at her shoes. Slightly worn heels.

"I never tell anyone my tiny tale of woe," she says. "I guess I'm still trying to apologize."

I lift my glass. "This renders you officially forgiven."

"You said two drinks."

"Okay, one more and then it's official."

She reaches for the bottle. I study her face as she pours into my glass. Her eyes are less alert, not so tightly focused. We toast again, this time without clinking glasses. The slivovitz has lost its chill. It still runs hot but now into my nose, the plum essence enhanced. At room temperature, it will probably go to our heads sooner.

The alarm on her cell buzzes. She walks to her desk, takes the pill canister out of her purse and swallows the psilocybin microdose.

"Yes, I know," she says without looking back at me, "probably not a good idea with the slivovitz... but just this once."

Returning to the sofa, she speaks in a far-off voice, as if continuing a confession of some long ago crime.

"I was about to give him a week," she says. "To clear out. I was right at the point of saying it, of shouting it. Then he suggested counseling, which made me hesitate. And then the cancer hit, which made me stop. Now I live in this matchbox."

I may not want our talk to veer off in Malcolm's direction, but if I'm going to tell her about his heart, this is the moment. Right now, it's hard to believe it would be like a dagger thrust.

"You were at the house the first time I visited," I say.

"I stop by to pick things up. Always when Yetta, the gardener or the security guy is there."

She leaves me hanging on this.

"What're you saying?" I ask. "That Malcolm can be threatening?"

She throws me a mocking glance. "He can be many things: persuasive, dictatorial, madcap, charming. In fact, he can be supremely charming, though you probably haven't seen that face yet. I've wondered what face he has been showing you in your sessions. He has an endless array."

My relief is turning to discomfort, but I feel obliged to give some reply. The sense of obligation makes me repeat and sound dull.

"So... you're saying he can put on a false face?"

"Expertly. Always on top of a false face already in place. I thought a trained therapist would see it immediately."

She regards me curiously, surprised or disappointed at my inability to distinguish the faces. I feel like we're back in the interview and I'm being grilled again. Except now she has hit a real sore point. My inability to see. I recall my last session with Malcolm, my sense that his cynicism disguises a yearning for oblivion. Like a mask over a veil, I tell myself, but now I can't be sure if I've returned to the insight on my own or if Beth has guided me to it.

"Watch him whenever he talks about Pacific House," she says. "Watch his expression. Watch his eyes if he doesn't hide them behind sunglasses." She either shivers or gives her body a shake. Probably the former, erased by the latter. "I don't want to talk about him anymore."

So don't start, I think, but I need to tell myself the same. What happened to my virtuous stance on client-therapist privilege?

"And I don't want to ask you any more questions," she says. "We've had enough for one day."

"No arguments there."

We act as if we have just quarreled and are now making up. Her thoughts scatter and I can no longer follow them. I become aware of the fog grown thick against the window. The time for me to leave must be drawing near, but she has dropped no hint. How can the fog be so heavy and solid, like a great wad of cotton pressed onto the glass? I remember reading that seasonal upwelling in the submarine canyon flushes deeper, colder water to the surface. Then gyres of warm Pacific wind hit the Bay and the air chills, condensing into mist. A chance to change the subject again.

"I thought it wasn't so foggy this time of the year..."

"It's fickle." She looks at the window. "There's that Sandburg line... What is it?" Her brow furrows and her spinal cord straightens. She turns academic, seeking a proper bearing to declaim. Her voice is controlled, precise, lovely: "'The fog comes on little cat feet. It sits looking over harbor and city on silent haunches and then moves on.'"

"Nice," I say.

It also seems to propel us miles away from our last

conversation. I return to my feeling of relief. I like being here in this old-world, fog-embraced cottage. Miles away from LA as well. Never to return. And when she isn't asking me questions, I like being here with this woman. I feel certain this cottage is a place where she can be herself.

She sits forward, brightens. "Should I read us something?"

"Sure," I say. What a fine idea. The fog, the sound of the waves, the fragrance of the plum brandy. Maybe I'll fall asleep right here on the sofa, drift off into vintage dreams.

She picks up a pair of glasses from the desktop, perches them on her nose. She approaches the shelves, begins to scan titles. I have glimpsed this side of her previously but now I get the full-on view. The fences are down and I've been invited into her world. Beth the abstracted scholar, the dedicated litterateur. She runs a forefinger over cracked spines, murmurs obscurely. "... shouldn't be here... have to change this..." She glances back over her shoulder, catches me looking at her legs.

"Do you know Jeffers very well?" she asks.

"Not really."

Not at all, would be more truthful. Why am I lying?

"Wait," she says. "Yes, okay, here we have some Czeslaw Milosz to go with the slivovitz. And then some Jeffers to wash down the Milosz." She returns to the sofa with a couple of texts, still on an academic roll, still mumbling. She says something about Milosz translating Jeffers and how Milosz's papers are held at the Beinecke Library at Yale. One day when she was a student, she thought she spotted Milosz in a hallway, but she was too terrified to approach him. "A great man," she says. "And I was a little Yalie." She flips through pages. "Wait, yes, good, here we are..."

She reads aloud some poems by Milosz. Her voice is natural and unforced, even more precise than when she quoted Sandburg. I ease back even further into the sofa. She makes short learned comments between poems, sometimes between stanzas. She says Milosz thought Jeffers "...opposed avant-garde fashions originating in French symbolism..." Her face in profile against the fog-pressed window. Dishwater hair draping her flushed cheek. Blue-green eyes bright, searching. I should have left twenty minutes ago. Now I'll never leave. The book is a bilingual parallel text. She says she will read a few lines in Polish to "honor the slivovitz," but she barely gets through one line—"*Więc starszy pastuch, skierdź, i torby jego...*"—before we both burst into laughter.

"He's describing an old shepherd and his bags," she says, still laughing.

"That's exactly what I thought," I say straight-faced, "but you made it sound Japanese."

She thrusts the book at me. "Okay, smart guy, you make it sound better!"

I mangle the same line and we laugh again. She opens another book, murmuring, "Yes, hmm, after she died....

and what a name—Una Call Kuster." She glances up at me. "I forgot all this," she says, "but how appropriate."

She "reminds" me that Robinson Jeffers and his wife Una lived for many years "just down the road." She says they were one of those "great literary love stories," and that Jeffers built Hawk Tower at Tor House for her, that he wrote, "I and my love are one." She adds, "You'd call it alchemical marriage, wouldn't you? The meeting of twin souls."

In the fog-heavy light, she does indeed dazzle quietly. I set aside my slivovitz. With painstaking slowness, I lean sideways across the sofa. I can't stop myself but my slowness gives her the chance to stop me, a chance to turn aside, pull back, end a thing before it starts. She has more than enough time to say, "Ryan, what're you doing? Please stop." But she says nothing. Maybe it's the psilocybin microdose. Maybe anything. I no longer feel relief. Now I feel I am about to plunge into a chasm. She can stop it. Instead, she doesn't even wait for my kiss to arrive. She meets me halfway. We fall together.

We both draw back. Plum brandy burns a bitter taste on my lips. I'm aware that I've just made a mistake, maybe a noble one, but a mistake all the same. I should say something, but can't find a word to mumble. Then she speaks and it is anything but a mumble.

"I'm not married," she says gloriously. "Maybe I never was. But I'm emphatically not. So don't let that thought enter your head. And I'm not anywhere but here. I'm not with anyone but you. I'm here now. With you."

Chapter Eleven

Two days later I receive an email from Beth. I hesitate to open it, fearing some reference to our lovemaking, some erotic phrase or amorous poem that could, in a court of law, constitute damning proof of my breach of all professional codes of conduct. A negligence-based malpractice suit isn't just post-coital jitters. Even a lenient judge would hang a therapist who sleeps with his dying client's wife.

I click open the email:

"Ryan, please find attached the transcript of our interview, slightly edited for content and clarity. Let me know if it meets with your approval. Sincerely, Beth Dijkstra"

I read it two more times. Obviously, she has avoided any possible reference to anything personal, exactly as I hoped, yet now I'm struck by the bizarre editorial reply. Cold to the point of creepy. Where is the woman who pressed her naked body against mine? *Let me know if it meets with your approval?* How can I even answer that?

I think back over our afternoon intrigue in *The Coast Quarterly* office. I ignored Malcolm when he said that "she dazzles quietly," that she has a "troubled mind." Now his words haunt and perturb me. The vintage sofa, the slivovitz, the alluring academic mumbling seductively as she searches for poetry. Did she really just stumble upon Robinson Jeffers and Una Call Kuster and their alchemical marriage? Maybe it was all orchestrated revenge sex. Or maybe I'm just going nuts inside the house.

I snap on my helmet and mount my bike. I glide down the hill, wheeling onto the coastal path like always but this time the Bay, the fog, the gray horizon, all the beauty, is fugitive, barely perceptible. I seek only to pedal away from my thoughts. I squeeze the contour handle grips, shift gears, pedal in strong swift strokes. I pass Breakwater Cove Marina, San Carlos Beach, the Hopkins Marine Station at Point Cabrillo. By the time I roll onto Lovers Point, sweat runs off my face. In the shore water, a group of scuba divers paddle toward a man in a kayak who directs them toward a kelp bed. Off the point, a lone surfer rides the break. A pair of sea otters bob on their backs beneath me, cracking shells on small rocks held on their stomachs. I watch them for a few minutes and something in me stops. Then I remount my bike and ride back into Monterey, back into my thoughts.

At home, I drink two glasses of water, shower, dress and read the transcript of my interview, which I barely remember. Are those really my words? My memory of the afternoon is limited to Beth's silken flesh, a scar near her left breast, her groans and pants in my ear, the fog against the window.

I open a beer, take a gulp and read the interview again.

Now, instead of being astonished, I see a professor in a stuffy classroom lecturing his students. Was I trying to transmit knowledge or just act like a kind old educator in bifocals?

A few more sips of beer and I calm down. The interview is not as godawful or ludicrous as I fear. I pretended to be who I was, that's all. Beth's questions might have turned a bit aggressive at the end, but they reveal my lost self, my forgotten soul. I begin to see again.

I send an email back to her:

"Beth, I have read the transcript of our interview, which you edited for content and clarity. Yes, it meets with my approval. Sincerely, Ryan Mathiesson."

I finish off the rest of my beer. In some way I do not understand, Beth's business-like email, the memory of intimacy, my bike ride, the two sea otters, my shower, and the interview transcript have compelled me to tell Beth about Malcolm's heart. It's like a cocktail that's been mixed and served. I have no idea how I came to the decision. I only know that now I must do it.

The following day one of Harry Higby's precepts comes potently to mind. *Unless we accept the consequences of our actions, we cannot purify, redeem and move on.* Yesterday I held the contour handle grips of my bike; today I hold the leather steering wheel cover of my car. I have managed to restrain mad impulse. I have not called Beth, even when every fiber of my being urges me to rush over to *The Coast Quarterly* office and throw my arms around her the instant she opens the door.

At the entrance to Pacific House, Yetta greets me and leads me through the mansion. The small library, the marble statuary, the billiard room. Something is different. What? There are pool balls on the table. We arrive at the kitchen and I pass through the sliding glass door, putting myself on guard. I must concentrate on the therapy session of a dying man. I cannot do or say anything that might hint at new emotions, let alone recent actions. I must keep Beth out of the conversation. If I pronounce her name, my voice will falter.

The Mexican gardener tips his baseball cap and I am slow to respond. If I am too friendly with the hired help, I may give myself away.

Engulfed in turbulent thought, I cross the entire field and approach Malcolm at the cliff edge before registering the day. There is no fog, the sky sparkles blue, the ocean is calm. It's a Los Angeles Hollywood southern California kind of day. Malcolm sits at the same small table by the flat granite boulder, but now in an electric wheelchair. He is unshaven and wears sunglasses. His right hand still holds the eagle's beak cane, but weakly. He tries to hide a wince of pain. His left hand rests near the wheelchair's joystick.

"So," he says without greeting, "how was your interview with my wife?"

My resolve to keep Beth out of the conversation didn't get very far.

"It went well enough," I reply flatly.

"What do you mean?"

"I suppose I could have given better answers."

"Did you tell her about my heart?"

"I've decided to tell her the next time I see her."

My tone sounds a final note, indicating we need not talk about this any further. But his left hand presses the joystick and the wheelchair whirrs to the left until he faces me directly. "And what did you think of her cozy Carmel office?"

"Nothing, really. I was concentrated on the interview."

"Come now, a few thoughts must have occurred to you. A fairy-tale Carmel cottage, classic Comstock architecture a stone's throw from the sea. Imagine the value of the place. Yet another prime parcel of land given by the Dijkstra Foundation to the penniless princess."

I can't shake the feeling that he suspects me from my toenails to my hair follicles. His every word feels like a probe. The dark glasses shield his eyes but I still detect a regal smirk. I sense him digging and burrowing into me. I warn myself it's only my nerves, my guilt. But maybe not. No matter how hard I try to avoid talking about Beth, for all I know, she could have told him herself. *After the interview, Ryan and I screwed for an hour or so. It was fun.* To teach a lesson, to exact some payback, to inject a bolt of adrenaline along with the psilocybin into her own eager veins. I don't know these people, I warn myself, don't know what lunacies either one of them might be capable of or what games they might be playing.

The sky is a bowl of blue silence above a tranquil sea. Tufts of wild grass along the cliff edge sway in a soundless breeze. A retreating wave hisses, sucking back sand on the beach below. I look at Malcolm and recall yet again that he is in the process of leaving all this—the silence, the breeze, the hiss of water on sand. But rather than bow before fate, he takes pleasure in opposing it.

"Where have you gone off to?" he demands.

"I'm here," I say, half truthfully.

"I thought therapists were supposed to maintain some focus in a session."

I get hold of myself and put an edge into my voice. "I always focus on why my client is saying what he says and how he is trying to acquire attention by saying it."

He smiles. The more uncomfortable he feels, the more assured he acts.

"Please turn off the tap on the New Age wisdom," he says. "Before we drown in it. And speaking of the ages, does the name 'Ohlone' mean anything to you?"

It is the same tone he used to ask about the eating habits of deer.

"They were an indigenous tribe, weren't they?"

"Correct." He looks over the field. I still can't see his eyes but his gaze lingers on Pacific House. He taps his cane on the ground. "They resided here before you and I, before anybody."

We are outside in crisp ocean air, but now he becomes the professor I was yesterday, the one in a stuffy classroom, transmitting knowledge accumulated by the past. He explains that the Ohlone Indians were the first natives of the Monterey Peninsula. They enjoyed a near boundless plenitude of nature. Their culture existed for some twenty, perhaps thirty centuries. Women planted seeds and gathered acorns. Men fished and hunted. "Rabbits, fox, grizzlies," he says. "And, of course, deer."

Then the Spanish arrived, he goes on, and began to set up forts and missions. The natives were astounded by these strange denizens from another world but they welcomed the newcomers and presented them with gifts, receiving, in return, marvelous cloth and beads. Before long the mission padres urged the Ohlone to accept the sacrament of Baptism. The Ohlone consented and, once baptized, found they had lost their freedom.

He either runs out of breath or feels a bolt of pain in his chest and I take the chance to cut in: "What're we doing here, Malcolm? Do you just want someone to listen to your stories or is there something else I can do for you?"

He ignores me, tries to catch his breath. At least we are no longer talking about Beth. He inhales a gulp of air and goes straight on. The padres held the Ohlone in the missions, he says, forcing the women to spin and weave cloth. The men were converted into slaves who tilled the fields. Spanish soldiers dealt with recalcitrants, employing manacles, shackles and whips. Overworked and beaten, enslaved and disease-ridden, the baptized Indians died off by the hundreds, all but vanishing from their once Edenic existence.

"I also have been baptized," he says. "By our modern-day missionaries, the doctors. They administer a sacrament they call 'prognosis' and I have lost my freedom to be alive. They christen me 'terminal' and shackle me to the fate of a 'pain management specialist'."

Again he taps his cane against the earth. I am about to insist that he tell me what he wants to accomplish by delivering this scholarly lecture but the cane stops me. Why does a man in a wheelchair need a cane?

"The missionaries always took the best land," he goes on. "Monasteries and convents, those institutions which espouse humbleness and poverty, are always sited on acres of priceless terrain. Likewise, the Dijkstra Foundation." Weakly, he waves the cane toward the field. "Ohlone shells and beads have turned up all over this yard. Security is tasked with frisking the gardener before he goes home at night. My wife wears Ohlone beads as if they are the crown jewels of her heritage rather than the dead souls of an exterminated people. Not jewelry, but genocide."

"Malcolm," I say, "this kind of thinking isn't helping you."

"Perhaps not, but it may help you."

"Help me?"

"To understand my wife. I warned you to beware of her dazzle."

I shift positions on the granite boulder. He has brought the conversation full circle back to Beth.

"I don't know what you're talking about," I say, but I recall the first note I made on him. *He fears tenderness.*

"No? Then tell me something. Did she read poetry to you on a foggy afternoon?"

I'm unable to hide a jolt of surprise.

"I thought as much," he says with disgust. "You who profess to know everything about alchemy. The all-aware therapist caught unawares." He shakes his head. "Very well, that's enough for one session. I have nothing else to say and it'll be best if you say nothing at all. But let me remind you that what passes here between us is confidential. If you are as noble as my wife seems to think, you will recall that our conversations are privileged. You are under a seal of confession. Just like the missionaries. Now please go."

He nudges the joystick and the wheelchair whirrs into a turn, leaving him staring at Pacific House.

CHAPTER TWELVE

"When you offered help," I say, "I know you weren't thinking along these lines."

"You've got that right," Jenny says. "Have you talked to anyone else?"

I shake my head. She is ill at ease and her discomfort embarrasses me. We sit on opposite sides of her desk. Her office is on the other side of the building, about half the size of mine, decorated in random disorder; folders and papers cover every flat surface. I glance down at my hands squeezed together on my lap.

"All my friends are in LA," I answer. "The ones I might unload on, and it's not something I want to talk about by phone."

She gives a look of comprehension. "I'm honored that you would confide in me," she begins slowly, "but professionally it's so far out of my day-to-day that I'm at a complete loss."

"Then don't speak professionally," I suggest. "Speak personally."

She stares at me, eyes wide open, lips pressed together. "None of it sounds good, Ryan. Even if your motivation was sincere at the start, you've gotten yourself into a situation that's so thorny you've come to ask advice from a virtual stranger."

"Does the stranger have any advice to give?"

"A traditional warning. Get out before you get in any deeper. Get out while the getting's good. You know what the lawyers always say: avoid even the appearance of impropriety." She regards me with concern. "I realize you're morally committed now," she goes on, "but it sounds like you can't even guess if one is trying to turn you against the other or which of them might be telling the truth or fabricating. So I have little idea of what to tell you, which is to say no idea at all. Have you been intimate with the woman?"

Intuition or smarts has guided her straight to the only salient detail I have withheld. And she has enough faith in her intuition or smarts to ask her question in a calm, judgment-free tone. She is what I used to be, a therapist who sees. I was reluctant to bring it up with her; now I feel foolish, stained, stripped bare.

"That's what you meant about my 'motivation'?" I ask.

"Go back to the day she told you about her husband's terminal illness. That was your chance to withdraw, to refuse to have anything to do with a situation you were unqualified for."

I can't keep my trap shut, can't stop from futilely defending myself. "It was also a chance to help someone, to turn my own life around, take a new direction. I don't know. Maybe I even succumbed to being flattered."

"If you had declined her request, you never would have seen her again."

My breath is cut short. "You're suggesting that subconsciously I agreed to help so that... I could stay close to the woman?"

"I have no way of knowing. It's just an impression. But from what you say, it sounds like the possibility was there."

I catch my breath but now my skin prickles as if I've ventured too close to flame. I need to get out of her office, get back to my own side of the building. I express thanks for her time, her discretion. I tell her that if she should ever need a favor, I'd be happy to return the kindness. I rise from my chair.

"Actually I could use a favor," she says, stopping me. "Are you free tomorrow?"

Her question is so unexpected I think I have imagined it.

"Tomorrow? Tomorrow's Saturday, isn't it? Wait, let me think. I guess I planned a bike ride, that's all. So, okay, yeah, I'm free."

"Perfect," she says. "I need a date."

One hundred white wooden chairs face a portable altar set beneath a flower-bedecked arch. Seagulls soar overhead and waves lap the nearby shore. The scene looks like a stage set—even the sun sinking toward the misted horizon—not quite real but not false either. Jenny and I join the other guests taking their seats.

"You must attend a lot of these," Jenny says.

"Not really," I reply.

Funny how many people think the same when even good friends avoid inviting me to their weddings. They apologize and hope I understand, but they fear I am like a jinx or a curse and that I will put a kiss of death on their magic moment. No one wants the slightest shadow of discord on a day of bliss and I inevitably augur the chance of trouble down the road. Likewise, who would want a mortician at a baptism?

The world is white. Bouquets of white roses surround the white altar. Snow-white lilies twine the lattice wedding arch. The guests wear white or pastel-colored sweaters and dresses. Even the mist coming in off the waves resembles drifting snow. I glance around. There are no bulldogs or playful kids but I think of the party at the child psychologist's house. Sitting next to Jenny helps summon the memory but like the party guests, these marriage people are virtuous and principled. Like Jenny, they are warm-hearted. There is nothing immoral, impure, unwholesome.

Did I take on Malcolm only to remain close to Beth? Since yesterday, I haven't been able to get the thought out of my head. I feel like I am crawling out of a deep coal mine. Coal dust speckles my face. My hands and arms are black. I must emerge from this strange dedication and lead a more natural life. I work for the collective, for these people here, but coal dust coats my lungs. I have no canary to carry down into the tunnels where I labor. Extraction, I think. I must bring to the surface the ancient remains of what once was living substance.

Yet maybe today I can give myself a break in the company of these people. The bride dressed in a white gown and the groom in a white tux stand barefoot in the sand before the altar. A Presbyterian elder pronounces vows. A few guests dab at wistful tears. The rumbling waves, the echoing bark of harbor seals and sea lions. As if scripted, the snowy fog drifts in off the Pacific and begins to cover the entire wedding party like a bridal veil. Is this a sacred ceremony, the uniting of twin flames, or just another impetuous grasp at a fleeting dream, soon to be snuffed out in divorce court?

I glance to the side. Gentleness graces Jenny's pretty face. Yesterday I needed to unburden myself and clear out my clouds. Today, unburdened but no better off, I wonder if I blundered. If I had called my dear friend and mentor Harry Higby, any ensuing chatter would have remained far south of Big Sur. So why didn't I call him? Simple. Besides the shame, I'm sick of LA reminding me I'm not who I was. Still, I don't think Jenny will spread salacious gossip all over the Counseling Center. She's not the type. But she is the type who might whisper in the strictest confidence to a friend, and that friend, also in the strictest confidence, might whisper to another. Only a matter of time before a group as large as this wedding party shares the same strict confidence, the same back-fence dirt.

She said, "I need a date." But I now realize she was really saying: "Ryan, you need a date. Let me take you to a nice place where you can be with nice people. You are damaged goods and it will do you solid to be in the presence of light and goodness. Distance yourself from confusion. Commit to your immaculate self. Have nothing more to do with that man and woman. They are trouble and you know it. Get out of the coal mine."

But no matter how it may appear from the outside, or how it may seem to Jenny or the good people assembled here on this beach, especially to the flames being twinned, I can think of nothing except what Beth said. She is not married.

Chapter Thirteen

I can't help but feel a little ridiculous. Minutes stretch into hours that feel like days, weeks, months since I made love to Beth. I buy flowers, I buy an assortment of cheeses, I buy wine I can't afford. Yet I know in my heart that slivovitz will remain our libation of choice, the offering we sprinkle onto sheets before slipping between them.

I remember her blue-green eyes, the oval shape of her nostrils, her long fingers and their mauve-lacquered nails. I remember her dishwater hair so well that I can visualize its exact dusty blond tone, feel the texture, the touch against my face. I know the caress of my palm on her waist, the sharp indentation at her ribs, like the marble curve of a statue. I remember her spurt of laughter as she read Polish poetry, her voice deepening as she murmured my name, her melancholic, erudite, abstracted air. I can recall all these details but I can't put them together and picture her. I summon Beth Dijkstra to mind and I see a feminine blur, an indistinct presence just beyond arm's reach. I ache to be with her again and, though absurd, the ache turns a day into a month.

Does this mean I believe she is my perfect lover, my twin flame? No, I'm not that crazy yet, but I have to admit I stopped acting normal a day or two ago. So now I shower, I shave, I make myself look as handsome as possible. At the last minute I decide flowers, cheese and wine are too much. I will smother her. So I leave the wine and cheese behind. The flowers might wilt. I drive halfway down the hill on Scott and turn back around. I leave the engine running, race into the house and come back with the wine and cheese. So what if I'm acting a little ridiculous? Where will bashfulness get me?

Besides, Beth has told me the staff has gone home and she will be alone. If she's not sheepish, why should I be? In Carmel, I park across the street from *The Coast Quarterly* office. The structure is similar to other fairy-tale cottages around town. The same undulating roof, fanciful stone chimney, flared eaves and hand-hewn timbered trim. But this one makes my heart thump.

Arms full, I approach the carved wooden door. Ring the bell or knock? A momentous decision. My eye lands on a small wooden plaque just to the right of the doorbell. All-heart redwood, sandblasted to accentuate its vertical grain. I didn't notice it before. Tastefully engraved lettering reads: *Dijkstra Foundation*.

I fumble with the flowers and wine. There is still time to take good advice and vanish. My forefinger draws back from the doorbell but too late as the door opens and Beth appears, dressed in a ginger-brown cardigan and printed silk skirt. All the distinct details—blue-green eyes, dishwater hair, long fingers—now snap into one thought: *It's her.*

"I come bearing gifts," I say, offering the flowers first, a dozen long stem, yellow and red roses.

She lights up. Her gaze leaps back and forth between the flowers and my face. Her smile is somehow modest yet avid.

"I can't even say 'You shouldn't have,'" she murmurs, "because I'm so happy you did."

She kisses me gently, then more passionately, crushing the flowers between us. Rose petals flutter down over her breasts.

"You look beautiful," I say, and almost add *dazzling* but instead say, "glowing."

"You make me feel it." She laughs. "Come in, come in. What will the neighbors think?"

My turn to laugh. Nothing businesslike or matter of fact about her today. I follow her inside. She closes and locks the door. We face each other in delicious hesitation. Will we make love this instant? No. Wordlessly, we opt to prolong the pleasure: meeting and greeting as foreplay. She runs water into a vase and I uncork the wine. We sit at a wooden table beside one of the fairy-tale windows. We toast silently. Raise glasses, soft clink. Our eagerness takes a pleasant turn, channels into everyday small talk. She tells me she has been editing a short story by a previously unpublished Sacramento writer who "thinks commas are periods," but who has "fresh and bold ideas." She says one of her great joys is coming upon a "gem in the slush pile."

Cornball to admit, but I would be agape if she were describing new cleaning products. I tell her a bit about the Garcias. I avoid using their name but still describe Mr. Garcia insisting on calling me a shrink. We share a chuckle. As I go on about clients, I'm tempted to ask how exactly she and Malcolm came to knock at my door. But better to keep Malcolm out of it. So I take a sip of wine and say I was beginning to think that Monterey marriages were problem free and lasted forever, but two new couples came in for preliminary sessions this past week.

Cutting cheese into bite-sized chunks, she listens, nods, looks up at me, alert and thoughtful. She arranges the cheese on a small silver platter.

"How do new clients normally come to you?" she asks.

"Mostly by word of mouth. Couples with problems seem to have friends who also have problems. Others arrive via my website or some internet forum where I've participated in a discussion. Sometimes I even get walk-ins—people in the middle of a bitter argument who pass by my office and spontaneously decide they need a referee." I set my wine down onto the table, no longer able to hold back: "How did you and Malcolm find me?"

The instant I mention his name, I regret it. Now he has taken a seat at the table with us. Beth sets a piece of cheese back onto the platter. She says that Malcolm found some website where I announced my forthcoming move to Monterey. He did additional research and then encouraged her to watch my Esalen talks.

"He said he was sure I would like your take on the mythology of relationships, your 'poetic understanding' of both couple therapy and classic literary couples. He was right, of course." She picks up the square of cheese again, regards it pensively and adds: "He's extremely good at reading people and discerning their desires."

I feel like the flowers have withered along with our conversation. We sit in silence. A minute passes, then two. Jenny was right: in deeper by the minute. Beth fixes her gaze on the cheese platter.

"I felt gaslighted," she murmurs, and then raises her voice. "I have no tangible proof. Nothing I can hold up as indisputable evidence. He's far too clever for that. But my intuition set off alarms. Too many casual conversations about the Dijkstra Foundation, about Pacific House, my family history. Too many odd feelings and strange emotions. Haven't you noticed how he makes you feel eerie, like something is creeping up behind you?"

"I'm sorry," I reply. "I can't talk about this. I made a mistake in bringing him up."

"I'm not asking you to reveal your private sessions," she says. "Just asking what you think. Does he seem normal to you?"

"Nobody seems *normal* to me," I answer evasively.

"Well, I felt oppressed and manipulated," she goes on as if I haven't said a word. Her tone heats up. "In a single month I went from being completely enthralled to feeling trapped and imprisoned, crushed by his implacable will."

"A month?" I drop a square of cheese. "You were only married a month? You never told me that."

"You said you didn't want to know. In the preliminary session you told us that our professions, social status, family background, time together wasn't important. You said all that mattered was that we had a marital problem."

"Yes, you're right, I know... but... one month. I mean..."

"I told you before: you can't imagine how charming he can be. It's like a by-product of how well he reads you. Unfortunately, I realized all this after the fact. After I had been courted, romanced, tickled pink, beguiled, swept off my feet and married. Too late, far too late. I also told you that I thought a trained therapist would spot it instantly. If you haven't, you can be sure he's reading and manipulating you every minute you're together."

I pour more wine, look out the window, watch a car pass by. Was it only a half hour ago that I was floating around sky high on the hope of making love? Beth isn't just venting. She's unloading grief, revealing a wound. Yet everything she says about Malcolm's charm isn't so different from him warning me about her "quiet dazzle." Did I agree to counsel him, as Jenny suggested, so I could stay close to her? Right now, I don't want to be near either of them.

"Like I said," I repeat. "I can't talk about this."

"You aren't," she replies. Her voice reveals a note of sorrow. "I am. You're listening. Who can I talk to otherwise?"

Point taken, but I sense it is the moment to end this. If we go on about Malcolm, the flowers will only wilt more. I suggest we go out for a walk to clear our heads.

"Good idea," she says.

But I have a hard time clearing my own head. My desire to make love now feels raw and futile. As we stroll down toward the beach, I wonder why, given everything she says, she doesn't throw Malcolm out of Pacific House. Why live in a fairy-tale shack instead of her rightful palace? Because, I realize, nothing has changed for her. She's still suffocated and morally trapped. Showing an obnoxious husband the door is one thing; throwing out a dying man quite another. And it doesn't matter anyway. In a very short time, death will simultaneously enact both divorce and expulsion from Pacific House.

A horn beeps softly behind us and we turn to find a gleaming Rolls Royce Phantom convertible gliding to a stop. A man sits behind the wheel, a woman in the passenger seat. Tanned, silver-haired, attractive couple. They wave to Beth and make me feel like I am back in Beverly Hills. The interior of the car is pristine white leather. A picnic basket covered by a red-and-white tablecloth rests in the back seat. Beth introduces me as "my friend, Ryan" and the couple as "some of our generous donors." I smile a greeting and they send back wider and whiter smiles.

Hollywood, I think. Executive producers. Power couple. But no, they merely represent local, Carmel-by-the-Sea wealth. I will the conversation to end but Beth goes on chatting about an upcoming art fair. It seems the couple own a gallery or a few galleries in town. They are involved in the fair and ask if Beth knows anything about the availability of a certain building. As she talks, she leans casually against the Rolls. I have taken a step back, careful not to touch the thing, fearful my belt buckle might scratch it. I think of Malcolm calling her a "penniless princess." Maybe true, maybe not, but her heritage shows from beneath her cardigan. She is accustomed to being near affluence, class, royalty. Drop her into brilliant society and her dazzle doesn't dim.

The couple drive off and we continue walking beneath the canopy of Monterey pine and cypress. We pass another fairy-tale house, this one with a driftwood fence. As we come out onto the beach, the magnificent view hits me adversely, the culmination of excessive splendor. Too many tea rooms, boutiques and gift shops in this town. Too many fancy cars and fake old world feel. The hanging flower baskets and carved weather-worn benches, the Cinderella courtyards and fanciful passageways, so rustic, so delightful. A perfect urban forest hamlet leading to a perfect white sand beach. Yet another Pacific sunset ready for a postcard photo. Maybe I just prefer scruffy Monterey, or more likely I feel a longing for even scruffier LA, where there are no dog-friendly beaches or storybook lives.

"Are you okay?" Beth asks.

Her question shakes me out of my funk. "Fine," I answer. "I just went away for a minute there."

Went away to my life. The town and beach, the Rolls and the sunset aren't what bother me. It's Malcolm, it's Beth.

We sit on the sand near a group of kids who are blowing soap bubbles. They have homemade wands fashioned out of coat hangers twisted into circles. Beth leans her head against my shoulder and we watch iridescent bubbles float by, listen to gulls squawk overhead. My feeling of gloom and futility begins to vanish with the bubbles. The kids are portraits of intense concentration. They pucker up and blow slowly to create larger bubbles. I watch their faces, thinking of the use of imagination, the value of fantasy. Perfect spheres of multicolored radiance, soap bubbles so soon evanescent, but these seem to last forever as they drift across the beach.

"It's because of cornstarch," Beth says, reading my mind. "You put a spoonful of it into the mix and it makes the bubbles stronger."

"How in the world do you know that?" I say.

"As a kid, I was crazy about soap bubbles."

It fits. Imaginative play foreshadows plenitude and I can picture her as a ten-year-old, her young mind full of exotic tales. A woman of letters in the making. My anxious thoughts evanesce with the bubbles. I turn my head and set my lips against her hairline, leave a kiss. I am at ease on this beach, in front of this ocean, with this woman.

"Let's go back," I say, "and see what happens."

Chapter Fourteen

Arriving home, I must take a nap. It is as if I have gorged on too much of everything at an enormous banquet. I feel bloated, weighed down, exhausted by excess. I collapse onto the living room sofa. My body needs quiet and relaxation. Yet there has been no large meal. I have consumed nothing but a few bits of cheese, a glass of wine. So what is it? Why this heavy load, this lassitude?

I stare up at the ceiling. I've never before looked at it, never stretched out on this sofa in this living room. Rest periods, siestas and coffee breaks. People have to withdraw within their sphere of selfhood, not only for rest but for dream and fantasy and soap bubbles. No one can sustain constant activity. We're not made for it. No matter the climate, no matter the city, whether LA or Monterey. The body and the psyche must absorb and dissolve free from external pressures. The need for recuperation. The need to digest. Holy hell, what am I going on about?

Sleep overcomes me. I doze fitfully for an hour or so. Then my cell phone rings. Grudgingly, I shake myself awake.

"Wha—?" I mumble.

It's Jenny, speaking in a worried tone. "I can't stop thinking about our conversation," she says. "I know I wasn't much help."

I roll up into a sitting position. I don't like the sound of this. "You were a big help. I was grateful just to have someone to talk to."

"I mean practical help," she replies. "So I was thinking that Frederick would be the person to go to."

"Frederick?"

"Frederick Kline."

Ah, now I get it. Perfect. Mister Squeaky Clean Kline, the official president of the Monterey Counseling Center, the representative of twenty therapists. The guy who wields a position nobody else wants, the guy who acts like the elected and glorified leader of a small nation. I was afraid she might whisper in secret confidence to a friend. Now she wants to make a public announcement to half the city.

"Like I said before," she goes on, "it's way out of my day-to-day, but Frederick's up on all that stuff."

"Stuff?"

"The ethics. The legal ramifications. I think it would be really useful if we talked to him."

We? "Listen, Jenny, I'm grateful for everything you've done—tremendously grateful—but please don't make this your problem. I'll take it from here."

"Of course. I didn't mean to butt into your business. It's just that you brought it up and I thought..."

"And I appreciate the thought. Really appreciate it, but for the moment I think it's best if..."

And so on and so forth and blah, blah. Jesus, hell.

Good people trying to do good things: they'll destroy the world.

Still half asleep, I go to the kitchen and brew some coffee. Time to wake up. Did I make myself clear? Should I call her back? I can't even remember what I told her. Oh yes, only the little detail that my dying client's wife is my new lover and bedmate. Staring hard at the coffeemaker, I think of how truly bad it sounds. And what sounds bad to me, will roar scandal and perversity to anyone else.

I have to drop what weighs on me. Not a heavy meal, but a heavy load. Jenny's right and I'm wrong. "Don't get in any deeper."

There will be repercussions, I know, but I should have banked on that from the start. Drop the load. Drop Malcolm. And tell Beth about his heart, yes or no. She'll find out soon enough anyway. Will she even care? Why haven't I told her yet—because I refuse to do Malcolm's bidding? Or because I'm just like Beth—afraid of him. Afraid of a dying man in a wheelchair.

I drink coffee. Yes, time to wake up. I have a business to run, bills to pay, new clients to think about. And the second part of the *The Coast Quarterly* interview fast-approaching. So I drink coffee and make notes on my clients, including a new treatment plan for the Garcias. After our last session, Mr. Garcia said if I had any more "shrink hours" open, he could recommend me to their friends. "If you think my husband's a looney," Mrs. Garcia added, "wait till you meet our cuckoo pals."

I answered that I would think about it. Now I'm thinking. How in need of work am I? Desperate, that's for sure, but not yet so rash and frantic and cuckoo myself.

Tapping at the keyboard, I hum aloud. Gradually, I become aware that it is not cheerful humming. I've joined the ancient song. I'm humming along to the mournful chorus of sea lions and harbor seals. Next, I tie up all my office-related work and turn my attention to *The Coast Quarterly*. I resolve that I have to do better this time. If I were truly noble, what would I see? What would I say?

I focus on the subject of the second interview, the metaphysics and poetry of alchemical love. Inevitably, I'll have to bring up great fictional and mythological lovers. Years since I last immersed myself in the literature but Romeo and Juliet have become so clichéd I can't imagine saying a single original thing about them. The same goes for Odysseus and Penelope. The faithful, long-suffering wife endlessly awaiting her hero-husband's return from the wars can't sit well with modern sensibilities, let alone the feminist readers of an avant-garde lit mag. So I settle on Psyche and Eros, Shiva and Parvati, Narcissus and Echo, Orpheus and Eurydice. Then I remember the book I bought. Abelard and Heloise.

I used to know these myths so well. Now I confuse names and events. I have to bone up on it all, not only the tales but the archetypes. I can't sound as if I just read all this material for the first time the night before the interview. I open boxes and come across old notes on Jung's divine union, on *hieragamos*, then more notes on the mystical marriage of Catherine of Alexandria to Christ; the spiritual betrothal of St. John of the Cross and Saint Teresa of Ávila; Herodotus on sacred marriage; Shinto wedding ceremonies; the symbolism of union and polarity in Tantric Buddhism. I spent years studying these texts, I tell myself, so I can't expect to re-absorb them in a single afternoon.

Then I come across a battered notebook devoted to Rilke. I used to adore the man. Not his poetry which I seldom understood, but his enormous correspondence, some 14,000 letters. At one point I grew determined to read them all, then the New Age came along and adopted Rilke as a type of self-help mystic and I set him aside. Now I recall how he wrote of communion with the sacred and transcendent and how I endeavored to emulate him on the communion of husband and wife. *Common union.* But no time to read all his letters before the questions begin.

In the first interview, Beth accused me of being cynical about marriage. She could turn aggressive again, revealing me as a sham. Of course, *The Coast Quarterly* isn't *The New Yorker*. That's why the interview is with me instead of some big name galactic star. They take what they can get. The circulation is small, the readership smaller yet. Half of the readers won't even finish the interview, just skim it to the end. The other half will forget whatever I say within an hour. But I don't fear exposure to a multitude of readers, only to one specific reader.

All of these literary names and amorous stories merely double my desire to see her again. Part of me—I don't dare call it my soul—radiates toward her. A moment later, as if by great cosmic coincidence, my cell phone beeps. A message from Beth. She told me she would contact me later so it's not so astonishingly momentous, but I'm still astonished. I read her message twice.

"Where are you? What're you doing? Let's get together, have dinner, go for a walk, talk, say nothing, say everything. Why spend so much time thinking about you when I can be with you? Let's meet. Let's make love."

CHAPTER FIFTEEN

Yetta admits me into Pacific House. Once again, I'm struck by its sheer size. Beth called it big and ugly. Maybe, but no matter. I'm determined that a different stage set awaits me. I've been walking circular paths. This house is like a machine and I'm a cog. We pass the sunroom, the library, the billiard room. Repetitive activity, continual patterns. Nothing will change until I do.

"So how are you today?" I ask Yetta.

She throws me a sideways glance. I can't tell if she fails to understand my English or if she's begging me to explain the events in this strange dwelling. Where is the mistress of the house? Where is the peace and serenity of a true palace? I have no answers. All I know is that I will not circle back this way. The hour of my departure is at hand. But instead of continuing down the hall into the kitchen and out the sliding glass door, she turns into a smaller hallway.

"Where are we going?" I say.

Again no answer, but this time it's not for lack of a language. She has been ordered not to speak. Threatened. I'm sure of it. When I repeat my question, she stiffens. We come to a large study. A rectangular window gives a view of trees. The opposite wall displays two small Rothko-like paintings. Or maybe they are Rothkos.

Malcolm sits in his wheelchair at a glass table. There is a large computer screen on the table. The sight of Malcolm in an enclosed space unsettles me. There is no roar of waves, no fog floating over us, no wind ruffling our clothes. He looks different than at our last session; his mouth hangs open and he has lost hair on the left side of his large head. Yetta scurries out and I double my resolve. This ends now.

"Today our session begins inside," Malcolm says. He waves his hand at the room, a gesture of ownership. He wants to show me that Pacific House is rightfully his. He made a similar gesture when he brandished his cane at the raging sea and referred to it as "savage, lawless nature." Maybe he thinks he owns it as well. How can anyone nurture such thoughts with death so near? He is hypnotized by himself, solely conscious of his own existence.

"That's fine," I reply, "because our session will be short today."

His eyes blaze. "I will decide its length."

"I'm afraid not." I take an envelope out of the inner pocket of my sport coat and slide it across the table to him. Not easy to part with it. My fingers twitch. His gaze falls on the envelope.

"What's this?" he says.

I am staring straight at him in his wheelchair but I experience the odd sensation that he is behind me. Ice on my spine.

"A refund," I say evenly. "I can no longer continue our sessions. This will be our last time together and I'm reimbursing you for—"

"I will decide if and when our last session takes place."

"That's already been decided, Malcolm. Quite truthfully, I never should have begun these sessions with you. It was my mistake." I have warned myself to keep explanations to a minimum but now I feel compelled to expound and justify. "I'm a marriage therapist and professionally I'm unqualified to handle your present needs. So I'm reimbursing you for the—"

"You gave me your solemn word," he says. He is about to smile, but then he coughs. "You told me you would be with me all the way."

"I know I did, but besides my being unqualified, other commitments have come up and I—"

He gives an ugly laugh. "*Other commitments.* You really do amuse me. So noble and dignified and now slithering out the back door. Did you really think I'd let you go so easily?"

I don't know how to answer him. His desire or chimerical itch to be in control is near constant. "Malcolm, listen to what I'm saying. It's not a matter of your letting me go. I'm gone. This is our last meeting. If you'd like help finding a replacement, I'll be happy to..."

As I continue, he breaks into a fit of coughing. He takes hold of the envelope, opens it, still hacking, and begins counting out bills. Before long I realize he's dividing the money in half. I'm still talking but he's no longer listening and gradually my voice trails off. He stuffs half of the bills back into the envelope and, still coughing, weakly flicks the envelope across the table toward me. He manages to bring his cough under control, but he struggles for breath.

"For your insolence and general stupidity," he says, wheezing, "I am cutting your pay in half."

Perplexed or dumbfounded—I'm not sure which—I stand motionless. I think of the note I jotted down after the preliminary session with Beth. *Deeply injured. Bleak soul.* This has gotten out of hand. I need to leave this house. I shake my head firmly, maintain an unyielding stance in front of him.

"You need help that I can't give. I'm very sorry."

"Perhaps I can convince you to reconsider," he says.

"That won't be possible."

"Well, let's try anyway."

He reaches for the mouse and activates the computer. The screen lights up. A photograph appears in which a man is handing a bouquet of roses to a woman. I flinch. The man is me. The woman is Beth. We are standing in the doorway of *The Coast Quarterly* office. It's the day I brought her flowers, cheese and wine. Malcolm stares at my face, inspecting my reaction. I sputter syllables which fall short of words. Before I can voice a coherent phrase, he begins clicking through more photos. One after another. Beth and I sitting on a bench by the sea, intently looking into each other's eyes. The two of us walking down the coastal path in Monterey. These are random, I think, out of chronological order.

Alarm and dismay come over me as more photos follow. The day Beth first mentioned the idea of doing an interview, the day I should have told her about Malcolm's heart. A photo of us parting ways that same day. We are only shaking hands but the affection between us is obvious. It looks more like we are holding hands, caressing. Then more photos yet. Kids blowing soap bubbles. Beth and I strolling down toward the beach. Chatting with the Rolls Royce couple. Walking beneath the canopy of Monterey pine and cypress, passing a driftwood fence, my arm around her. Sitting on the beach. Beth leaning her head onto my shoulder. For every photo someone had to be standing behind us with a camera and telephoto lens. Why didn't I turn and look?

Then comes a shot of me leaving a kiss on Beth's forehead. Followed by the sun sinking into the Pacific, the sky aglow.

"This is quite lovey-dovey," Malcolm says.

I stammer but still can't voice a word. He begins hacking again, as if the photos are the real cause of his disease.

"Now for the juicy stuff," he says.

He clicks the mouse and a new photo appears. Another shot of Beth and I in the doorway of *The Coast*

Quarterly office. This time we are kissing, the rose bouquet crushed between us. Rose petals fluttering down over our feet. Malcolm clicks onto a new photo. A street view of *The Coast Quarterly* office, one of the fairy-tale window. Followed by a closer shot of the interior taken through the window. Beth and I seated at the wooden table, raising wine glasses, gazing at each other. We toast. I can almost hear the faint clink of our glasses. It is the moment before Beth said, "You can be sure he's reading and manipulating you every time you're together."

Now four or five photos of Beth and I walking from the beach back toward *The Coast Quarterly* office. In the middle of the tree-shaded street, we share a passionate kiss. My pulse begins to race. Every moment of our evolving affair is documented here. But the shots are out of sequence again. What is this madness? My breathing sounds like gravel spilling out of a metal bucket. A shot of us entering *The Coast Quarterly* office. Through the fairy-tale window again. Beth and I near the vintage sofa. A dozen shots in quick succession of us undressing each other. Then I stand naked, my erect penis in Beth's hand.

"My, my," Malcolm says. "Such eagerness."

I feel like all the air has been vacuumed out of my lungs. A dozen, maybe two dozen photos follow. Beth and I making love on the sofa. Shots of every position imaginable. I am shocked by our nakedness.

Whoever took the photos had to be standing right outside the window, telephoto lens against the glass. It is like viewing cheap homemade porn. I feel enraged, disoriented. Above all, I am frightened. Where is this perversion leading?

I tear my eyes away from the screen and stare at Malcolm in cold dread. He gazes back at me in amusement.

"Pick up your pay and follow me," he says.

Chapter Sixteen

Malcolm guides the wheelchair along a worn path toward the cliff edge. I follow behind him. The Mexican gardener pretends to be busy bundling twigs as we pass. The ground is smooth along this route. The wheelchair barely bounces but I stumble. I am rattled. I need to make my mind think. In front of me, Malcolm's large head and the ocean whirl. The sky is black.

Malcolm couldn't have known I was going to stop our sessions today. I hardly knew it myself. On the drive out here I was still deciding. So the photographs are part of some other plan. He adapted them to the surprise of my telling him this was our final session. He has invented a game, made the rules, knows what's at stake and also knows—or thinks he knows—when the game will end.

We come to the cliff edge and I take my seat on the flat granite boulder. Malcolm steers the wheelchair around. Today, the fold-out table is not here. The sea is gray and choppy but unmarked by the raging waves I expect to see. A fishing boat, maroon or dark green, makes for the horizon. There is a buzzing in my head. Some force has been released, elemental or archetypal. The surge of the water and the waves. Jenny had it wrong. She said I had gotten myself in too deep. Not deep, but far. I ventured too far from shore. Now the danger of shipwreck. The link between my small self and the vast ocean. Like a boat landing after a storm, I will need reconstruction. How is it that I didn't see whoever took the photos? Easy answer. I never once looked over my shoulder or even glanced to the side. My eyes were fixed on the object of my desire.

"Make yourself comfortable," Malcolm says. "We still have much to discuss in today's session."

I find my voice but it is weak. I sound like I am whining. "Malcolm, I don't know what you think you're doing here but..."

He coughs twice. "Try to pay attention. Concentrate and listen. That's what you're being paid for." He looks back at Pacific House. "And no more acting like a strong-arm therapist. The time to put a stop to things was ten minutes ago. You could have said bye-bye, marched out the front door with your nobility intact and driven your medium-priced car back into normal life. You didn't because you're afraid. You know that normal life no longer exists for you."

I still need to make my mind think clearly but his sarcasm and hostility clash against my ear. Besides everything else—the shock of the photos, the panic they engender—something is wrong here. The dark green fishing boat becomes a dot on the gray sea, silhouetted against the horizon. I sense he's going to talk about Beth. Trapped and imprisoned, crushed by his implacable will: that's what she said, that's how she felt.

"First of all," he goes on, "my dear wife knows

nothing of all this. So for the moment we will keep it to ourselves. Our little secret, let's say. Besides, it might upset her. Her tender sensibilities. She is a romantic not only at heart but in her liver, her feet, her genes. It forms part of her heritage. It has been handed down to her along with everything else." He looks again across the roll of land toward the house. "Can you even guess the value of this property?"

He stares at me, demanding an answer. I continue to detect a discordant note. Not in what he is saying but in how he is saying it. How much he is saying. The wordiness, the detail, the long phrases. I should keep my mouth shut but can't hold back.

"A million dollars," I say sharply.

He laughs, coughs, struggles to catch his breath.

"Maybe the postage stamp of dirt we sit on here," he says, "but I assure you the rest of the estate is worth a few pennies more." He casts an eye across the land as if conducting a formal appraisal. "The Dijkstra Foundation specializes in snatching up prize immoveables. They thrive on equity, and exult on dominion and proprietorship. Old world wealth brought to bear on American soil. Meanwhile my wife pretends her last name is Smith or Jones."

He shakes his head, coughs violently. So much talking has exhausted him, I think. A body wracked by illness needs quiet repose, gentle breathing. Instead he engages in prolonged remarks, excessive effort. Is it only rage and gall? I think he can't go on, but then he does:

"I am an American success story. I am a millionaire. I did not and will not inherit a dime from my forebears. I worked hard and pulled myself up by my proverbial bootstraps. No one gave me a minute of time let alone a mansion of infinite space. Tell me, mister therapist, what good is it to be a millionaire if you can't buy what you want?"

Again I can't keep my mouth shut. "I'm not here to consult on your real estate fantasies."

"You are wrong," he replies. "Very wrong. And if you think that by sleeping with my wife you will gain some future right to this house and land, you are wrong about that as well."

Now I can keep my mouth shut, but only because his inane comment leaves me with nothing to say. Again I'm annoyed at hearing *my wife, my wife*. Drumming the words into my head. Never once calling Beth by name.

"Now let's discuss my wife's equestrian skills," he says. In a monotone he goes on to tell me Beth has been riding horses since childhood and she is presently a member of the Pebble Beach Equestrian Center. "She has highly developed equestrian skills," he emphasizes. "As a result, she has highly developed thighs. Years of training and constant use have made them sleek and muscular. More to the point, she knows how to use them. She knows how to put the squeeze on a man."

Vulgarity layered on top of homemade porn. He is trying to disgust me. He wants to knead my emotions into a soft dough he can better manipulate. Or that's what I conclude, but I sense the vulgarity isn't put on. It's one of his faces, attached to some erotic kick he gets out of being vulgar. And again, lengthy speech. What fuels his rancor? Even hatred has limits. I still fear where all this is heading, but I won't dignify his filth with a show of repugnance.

"You and *your wife* are separated," I say. "She's your ex-wife."

"Who says that? You? My wife? Certainly not any legal or official entity. I know only that she has been working late at the office. The pressure of publishing those pesky poems. Imagine my shock when I learn she and my loyal therapist are engaged in wanton acts of sensual embrace. I am distraught. The man to whom I entrusted my mental health is making me mentally ill. This being America, I have one obvious course of action. I'm obliged to sue."

"You won't get far with that."

"My lawyer thinks otherwise."

He reaches into a side pocket of the wheelchair and brings out a dosette box and a small bottle of water. He takes two pills, drinks, swallows, returns everything to the side pocket. A normal action for any sick person, except I suspect he hasn't gulped down aspirins for a headache. Nor has he taken a psilocybin microdose or any drug prescribed by his oncologist or cardiologist. Amphetamines, I'm sure of it. Whizz, crystal, some street upper. Terminal illness slammed on his brakes but he won't let a little thing like that stop him from getting what he wants. Even if it loads more stress onto his already failing heart. So he sends an adrenaline-like charge into his central nervous system. He's energized, alert, chatty.

"My lawyer says that no serious business on earth likes to be sued," he goes on. "It doesn't matter by whom or for what. It makes for bad business. She believes she can prove the Monterey Counseling Center did not hold itself to the code of behavior it espouses in its charter, the so-called 'ACA Code of Ethics'. They were more interested in renting office space than doing a background check on a morally corrupt therapist. Imagine what your colleagues and patients might think if I invite them to view some photos. Then, of course, there is the more clear-cut matter of a malpractice suit against you personally."

He breaks off into another fit of coughing. I pick at some lint on the sleeve of my sport coat but I am play-acting and he knows it. I am concerned with a lot more than lint. There is no longer any denying that I am out to sea and no boat landing in sight. Nowhere to moor emotions. Fresh ocean air and I can barely breathe. Time to forget about all his talking. I need to focus, think straight, act. He brings his hacking under control.

"In Monterey," he says, "a decent lawyer who will defend you from these allegations, someone fairly competent but not very brilliant, will cost you five thousand dollars. That's merely to walk in the door and get him or her started on your case."

"I don't have a case," I reply, "and you wouldn't waste your money."

"No waste at all. My lawyer is on retainer. She has been sitting around doing nothing for months and now it's time for her to earn her keep. By the way, she is a shark and she chews people into bits. When she starts chewing on you, you will see that you do indeed have a case."

I can't take any more of this. I feel shot to pieces, powerless.

"What is it, Malcolm? Why are you doing this? What do you want?"

He stares at me and in his gaze I behold what I should have seen before. Or noticed that I was not seeing. There is no trace of humanity. Rather, I behold an indwelling demon veiled by a false smile on a new face. He raps his cane against the base of the granite boulder. "Are you comfortable sitting there?"

When I make no reply, he goes on:

"For the moment, we will continue our sessions just as before. You will come here as agreed, and you will listen to whatever I have to say. You will also continue to screw my wife and if she asks about our sessions, you will tell her that things are going fine, nothing more."

"She won't believe me."

"Then tell her you are prohibited from saying anything by your ACA confidentiality and privacy agreement. Specifically, Sections B.1.a to B.1.d. Have you read them recently? Perhaps you should. Meanwhile you will slowly but surely get your hands on my wife's contract agreement with the Dijkstra Foundation in regard to Pacific House and its property. She keeps it somewhere in *The Coast Quarterly* office. I want that information."

I look at him aghast. "What do you mean—sneak around her office and pry open drawers?"

"Precisely that."

I shake my head. "There is no way on earth I will ever do that."

"Then I will bring you down. One warning and down you go." He waves his cane weakly over the yard. His tone changes, as if we are two old friends recalling past pleasures. "Do you remember when we spoke about the Ohlone—the indigenous tribe who once occupied this land? They used to dance on this very spot where we now sit, not a *marriage dance,* but a dance to celebrate a war victory or to bring forth rain, fortify the soil and encourage plentiful harvests. Perhaps to protect against illness and earthquakes. Perhaps..." He waves his cane at the sea. "... to keep chaos at bay."

More talking. More acceleration. He acts as if he's delivering a lecture to an anthropology class. He points the cane at a gulch near the side of the property, halfway back to the house. "Long ago a *temescal* stood there. An

Ohlone sweathouse. Prior to a hunt, the Ohlone men gathered around a fire and sweat until their bodies and minds ran clean, removing every human odor and impure thought. Then they made a sacrifice."

Again he taps his cane against the base of the granite boulder. "Still comfortable?"

I feel myself sliding backwards. Originally, I came here to give peace of mind and now my own mental tranquility has all but vanished. I wonder if he ever had the vaguest desire to heal. He continues tapping his cane against the boulder. I sense in him a yearning for oblivion.

"This stone was very important to the Ohlone. It served as their altar of sacrifice." His dark eyes observe me. "Yes," he says. "I will not hesitate to sacrifice."

Sitting motionless on the boulder, I feel a chill rise into me. I shudder.

He taps the cane one last time. "That ends our session for today."

Chapter Seventeen

I see no alternative but to tell Beth everything immediately, so I drive for Carmel and *The Coast Quarterly* office. We'll figure out a way to handle the mess. Malcolm's threats are empty anyway. He'll be dead long before his shark lawyer can start to nibble let alone chew me into bits. Besides, I am not about to be bullied by an unhinged psychotic. I should have told him to get fucked and left it at that.

I turn off Highway 1 and enter Carmel on Rio Road. Minutes later I find I'm on Ocean Avenue but I can't remember what route I took to get there. The fairy-tale shop fronts appear grotesque, as do tourist smiles. Everyone is moving in slow motion. I turn left. A block from *The Coast Quarterly* office, I pull the car over and cut the engine. A sharp tingle of premonition runs through me. I check the rear view mirror. Normal street scene. Some pedestrians, some light traffic, a dark blue car fifty yards behind me. Maybe I didn't tell Malcolm to get fucked but I can tell him right now. Click on the phone, hit the speed dial and speak the words into his perverted skull.

But I still hear his question echoing in my own skull. *When was the last time you read the 'ACA Code of Ethics'?* The answer: so long ago I didn't even remember the title. How smoothly he referred to the confidentiality and privacy agreement, as if he reads it every morning over breakfast. "Sections B.1.a to B.1.d." Then bacon and eggs sunny side black. He is no longer just projecting anger. If he ever did for real. Now he aims it like a weapon. I still feel the chill of the granite boulder.

I warn myself not to do anything rash. That's exactly what he would want. Me flying off the handle and acting crazy while he stays on target, callous, calculating. I re-start the engine, scan the rear view, drive past *The Coast Quarterly* office and set off for Monterey.

Fisherman's Wharf rests in the spell of a quiet day. I sit on a bench and watch seagulls drift by overhead, swoop down over glittering ripples. The moaning of sea lions and harbor seals. Not much fog. As ships enter and leave the harbor, I notice a man in a battered yacht captain's cap. The gold embroidery and anchor emblem have faded to a dirty yellow. His white hair sticks out from under the cap. He has the look of a retired sea captain, observing the come and go of ships. An experience in which he was once deeply involved. I picture him sailing his ship through fierce storms. Maybe he has attained quietude. A mind beyond struggle and victory.

Of course, I fantasize all this, but it helps calm me down. I begin to think more clearly. I admit that part of what Malcolm said was true. Like any Janus-faced psychopath, he knows the value of a good lie, a half truth. Yes, Beth is romantic. And I've caught her on the rebound. A romantic woman in a fouled-up divorce, wanting nothing except escape, freedom at any price. And I waltz into a relationship with her. Not very smart, not very well planned. I know all this and I understand it and I also know I don't care. Don't give a good god damn.

What Malcolm doesn't comprehend, will never comprehend is that romanticism isn't unrealistic, syrupy mush. That's only the version his cynicism creates. It has nothing to do with a profound appreciation of beauty, an exaltation of truth and, yes, nobility.

Thinking these thoughts, I watch my mind scatter in a dozen directions and I realize I can't possibly submit to a second interview for *The Coast Quarterly*. Not now. Not in that office. How could I ever sit there in tranquility and not think about prying open drawers? Maybe that's what Malcolm really wants. To throw me off, ruin the interview and make both Beth and I appear ridiculous. Punish us for turning him into a cuckold.

An elderly woman with a cane approaches the sea captain. They talk briefly and then stroll off together. The sight of the aging couple holding hands reminds me with a start that I have a 5 o'clock appointment with the Garcias. I completely forgot about it. Thank the foggy skies I decided to come into Monterey. I could be talking wildly with Beth right now and losing patients is the last thing my frayed pocketbook needs.

I walk to the Counseling Center and arrive fifteen minutes early, more than enough time to review my notes on the Garcias and focus on their case. As I enter the building, leaving behind the song of the sea lions, Shirley signals to me from Reception. I approach her and say hello. She replies that Frederick wants to see me.

"What about?" I ask.

She pulls a face. "What's it ever about with him?"

In his office, Frederick acts no different than he did at the child psychologist's party. Formal, correct, stiff as a mop handle. The supreme president of the Counseling Center. He rises from behind his desk. He is dressed in a dark blue blazer, cream-colored shirt and maroon tie, the only staff member who doesn't wear a sweater and jeans. He advances, dutifully shakes my hand and, in his official voice, announces that half an hour ago he received a call from a woman who identified herself as a lawyer. The woman asked to meet with him on a matter concerning me.

"Her name..." He reaches back to his desk and picks up a paper. "...is Ms. Susan Colburne. Know her?"

Struggling to appear perplexed, I shake my head. "What did she want?"

"She said only that it was a serious matter and inappropriate to discuss over the phone. We agreed to meet on Thursday."

"No idea," I say, "but if you want me to be there, just say the word."

We shake hands again and I walk back down the hall. As I pass Reception, Shirley looks at me with curiosity and I nod to her amicably. No problem, nothing at all, just a normal chat with Frederick, a normal day here at the Center. I open the door to my office, enter, close the door and lean back against it, taking in a sharp breath. So Malcolm didn't waste any time. A shot fired across my bows. *One warning and down you go.* He has turned loose the shark who chews people.

The Garcias arrive on time and in the middle of an argument. I welcome them, usher them toward the triangle of chairs, take my seat and begin the session on automatic pilot, acting out my role as I feverishly think of what I must do to avoid being chewed. *You will continue to screw my wife.*

"It isn't about talking," Mr. Garcia says at one point. "It's about too much talking. She doesn't stop talking. Talking, talking, talking."

"Maybe you should start listening," Mrs. Garcia says.

"Okay, good," I say, switching off my automatic button. "Let's pause here for a moment. We know this type of bickering doesn't lead us anywhere. Maybe we can look at the 'why' behind it."

I manage to take the edge off the session but I'm still on edge myself. In the swirling chamber of my head, I continue to hear the same phrase. *Are you comfortable sitting there?* A moment later I realize that Mr. Garcia is shaking his own head. He looks as if someone has just tweaked his ears. He encases me in a significant look and says:

"Maybe the fancy shrink word is *bicker* but the real word is *argue*. And that's all I do here. So I'm beginning to wonder why I'm paying your high prices. I can argue for free at home."

He throws a nod of satisfaction at his wife, as if to say, *Think about that, sweetie.* Then he looks back at me, confident that I have never in my career been challenged by such a sharp-witted statement. His pride is brazen. I appear to lend his words serious deliberation. Then I offer my standard reply, given a hundred times in the past.

"Mr. Garcia, your free arguments at home are outrageously expensive. They are leading you step by step to emotional and spiritual bankruptcy. That's why you came to see me in the first place. You're here because you don't want to go bankrupt."

He observes me with large white eyes, lower lip trembling. He looks at his wife. She looks back at him. They stare at each other in silence. Then Mrs. Garcia says:

"Remember on the way home we have to pick up some milk."

The session ends a short while later and they leave still seething but no longer in open battle. Improvement, I tell myself.

An hour later at home I realize that my phone has been switched off since I left Malcolm. I was going to switch it on in the car by *The Coast Quarterly* office but then didn't. Now I find two text messages and a voice mail from Beth. She asks where I am and when we will next get together. She sends hugs and kisses, both written and spoken. As far as I can tell, her tone of voice is normal, not at all agitated. I start to call her but then stop. I have to tell her to postpone the second interview but I have no idea what else to say.

CHAPTER EIGHTEEN

The following morning, another text message arrives from Beth, this one without any hugs or kisses attached. Just two words and a question mark. *What's up?* I reach for my car keys, convinced I must go over to *The Coast Quarterly* office and tell her everything. Then I think better of it. I consider calling Jenny but sense big mistake. So I call Harry Higby, my mentor, the man I should have called from the start. When he comes on the line, I apologize for not calling sooner. As I go on to describe Malcolm and his threats, a rivulet of sweat runs down my back. I reveal that my dying client's wife—or ex-wife—is my lover. Three hundred miles away and I feel Harry draw back from the phone.

"To begin with," he murmurs, "you better do what the guy suggests and reread the Code of Ethics. Actions have consequences, Ryan. You know that. Unacceptable principles and established order don't mix." His voice trails off, comes back strong. "What you're describing sounds like more than just personal recklessness. There's some kind of unconscious pressure or inner upheaval going on. If you can't see it, you need to get into therapy yourself. Other than that, all I can say is you've got to face facts."

He makes no attempt to hide his shock and disappointment. I thank him and say goodbye. His own goodbye is cheerless, heavyhearted. I feel like I've been placed under arrest and tossed in the clink. I sense someone else in there with me. The authorities have taken two men into custody. Me and my former self.

I pace back and forth across the living room, the phrase *If you can't see it* still in my head. It seems to proclaim that I really am going blind. The only thing I still know for certain is that I have to cancel the second interview. I can't deal with it and survival at the same time. So I text a message to Beth. Something unexpected has come up. No big deal, just super busy. Get back to you soon. Hugs. Kisses.

I pull a box of old papers out of the closet, dig through documents, toss stapled files onto the sofa, onto the floor. Eventually, I come across a pamphlet. The ACA Code of Ethics. Sections B.1.a to B.1.d. Confidentiality and Privacy. I can't remember ever reading it before. Maybe I did years ago, back in Esalen days. I skim paragraphs, snatching up words like hot coals. Trust. Upholding boundaries. Disclosure of information. Respect. Limitations. Breached.

I skim faster. Harmful relationships. Ethical violations. I'm skimming not to take in more information, but out of fear of what I'll read. I go back twenty pages and force myself to slow down. Section A.5.a. is titled "Sexual and/or Romantic Relationships Prohibited." No surprises here, no back door I might slip through. Never mind steamy-in-the-flesh sex, the Code of Ethics even prohibits "electronic interaction" with any relative or family member of a client for "5 years following the last professional contact."

So that does it. No matter how blind I might be, one thing I can't fail to see is bankruptcy. Not the spiritual kind I sketched out to Mr. Garcia, but insolvency. Every last dime sucked out of me in legal fees and fines. Any normal judge might even consider a short prison term. Especially with Malcolm in court in his wheelchair, putting on an anguished face, a cancer victim turned into a cuckold by his amoral therapist.

I warn myself not to engage in manic thinking. Give the mind permission to run off into crazyland and it'll do exactly that. I need to remember that this is twenty-first century United States of Annulment. Thirty or forty years ago eyebrows might have jerked upwards over a licentious love affair, but now? My patients alone could fill hundreds of court briefs with their extracurricular activities. Who hasn't had or doesn't know someone who has had an affair? Nowadays, even priests stand in long lines to the confessional.

I'm about to drop the Code of Ethics back into the box when my eye hooks onto the title of another section. Boundaries of Competence. Therapists may only practice within the areas defined by their credentials, professional experience and training. I imagine a judge asking me to explain what qualifies a marriage counselor to treat a terminal cancer patient.

The feeling of being arrested and tossed in the clink returns. Once more I prowl the living room. Back and forth, back and forth. Step by step, I resolve to fight for all I'm worth. I won't let Malcolm Favor or his shark lawyer browbeat and terrorize me. If they want to mix it up, okay fine. Bring it on. They'll get a few surprises.

These brave thoughts thrill me for two minutes. Then I collapse onto the sofa and stare my sorry plight square in its ugly eye. While I'm squirming and fighting for my life, Malcolm can gaze peacefully over the ocean, glancing at a sacrificial boulder, giving new instructions to the shark: "Squeeze him until he bleeds pennies."

My only prayer is that he dies sooner rather than later. So I can't delay any longer. I have to talk to Beth. She'll know what to do, or at least have some idea of how to handle her ex-husband. Together we can solve this.

I leave the house. Before getting into the car, I send a text message. "On my way!" I can't think of anything else to add. Then I decide it's better to add nothing. Nothing that might later be admissible in a court of law. Though whoever heard of a text message being admitted into evidence because of the word *darling* or *honey*?

I command myself to calm down and drive slowly. My eyes dart at the rear view mirror. Am I acting like a fool? Or, given the circumstance, am I behaving with discernment? I'd be foolish not to look at the rear view. I don't fear my own shadow but rather the shadow following me.

Then I recall that I signed some similar code of ethics with the Monterey Counseling Center when I joined the team, promising never to engage in any activity that might bring disgrace onto me or my fellow therapists. So forget about a court of law. One glance at the juicy photos and Squeaky Clean President Frederick Kline will put my office up for rent.

In Carmel, I park the car and remind myself. *Together we can solve this.* I head across the street to *The Coast Quarterly* office. Beth meets me at the door, kisses me full on the lips. I pull back, anxious over a new doorway photo. She notices my faltering but addresses me eagerly.

"Wait until you hear the quote I found from Rilke. I've just been translating it."

"You— you speak German?" I say, following her inside.

"Only enough to get myself in trouble. But MaryAnn speaks enough to get me out and between us..."

A voice chimes in: "...it was no trouble at all!"

In front of me, a short dark woman springs up from behind a desk.

Beth says: "MaryAnn Baros, I'd like you to meet Ryan Mathiesson."

The dark woman reaches out and shakes my hand enthusiastically.

"I copyedited your first interview," she says. "It was excellent. The harmony."

"Harmony?" I say.

"Between you and Beth. We're all looking forward to Part Two."

I become aware of another person in the room, Bernie, the twenty-year-old intern. He waves from near the photocopier. I follow Beth to her desk and sit opposite her. I thought I would experience relief in her presence but I still feel locked up behind bars. I can't utter a word while MaryAnn and Bernie are nearby. Against my will, I glance around, wondering where the contract agreement with the Dijkstra Foundation might be hidden. *One warning and down you go.*

"Listen to this," Beth says. "'In a good marriage each person appoints the other to be guardian of his or her solitude...'" She glances up, smiles. "'... thus they show the greatest possible trust to each other.'"

MaryAnn comes up behind me, adding: "It really jibes with some of your thoughts in the first interview, Ryan."

I swing my head halfway around. "I guess... it does..."

"We're considering sprinkling similar quotes throughout the issue," Beth adds.

I've barged into *The Coast Quarterly* office on a typical workday, so what did I expect? Bernie wanders over, sits on the edge of a desk. His dumb, happy grin discharges delight: he spends long hours in a fairy-tale dwelling with two older attractive women. Beth reads other quotes and the three of them make observations, exchange comments, invite me to comment.

Observing Beth, I wonder if she resides in this cozy box instead of her spacious mansion to punish herself for having married Malcolm, for having bought whatever face he sold her. I also wonder if she's on a cloud-nine high right now thanks to a psilocybin microdose or just cheery. Will we solve this together?

"We could juxtapose Rilke with an opposite," she says. "Listen to this from Pessoa." Her voice deepens. "'How wearisome it is to be loved, to be truly loved! How wearisome to be the object of someone else's bundle of emotions!'"

MaryAnn and Bernie laugh. I can't even rouse a chuckle. They reach some conclusions and MaryAnn returns to her desk, Bernie to the photocopier. I convince Beth to go out for a walk. I'm still determined to tell her everything but once out the door she takes my arm and I grow nervous.

"What's wrong?" she asks.

"What do you mean?"

"You've been acting weird since you arrived."

"It's what I texted you. Something unexpected came up. I've still got it on my mind. Nothing important."

My first lie to her. It feels wrong and shameless; worse yet, she doesn't buy it.

"It's Malcolm, isn't it?" she says. "What did he do?"

We come to the beach. No soap bubbles today. We sit on the sand. I again worry about being seen together publicly, but what does it matter if someone is taking more photos? They can't be any worse than the ones already taken. I rest my hand on her leg, recalling Malcolm's vile words. *It's quite the ride.* The unmistakable proof that I've gotten in too deep is how deep he has gotten into me.

"If you can't tell me because of client privacy," Beth says, "okay. If you can't because of fear, that's not okay."

Breakers dash white foam across the shore. The ocean heaves. I remove my hand from her leg.

"MaryAnn knows me quite well," she goes on. "She always says she thinks I attract lovers with problems. Maybe it's true. Repeated patterns usually mean an excess of something. But I broke the pattern of my marriage to get the hell away from Malcolm and I sure don't want him here with us. So if he is, I'd like to know why."

I can't manufacture a reply. Even here in front of the ocean, me and my former self remain jailed in a cage. Today Beth and I aren't going to solve anything together. We sure won't go back to *The Coast Quarterly* office and make love. If I don't do something soon, we may never make love again. Ironically, it means I'll also disobey Malcolm's command: *You will continue to screw my wife.*

"I don't like this," Beth says.

I feign ignorance. "Like what?"

"This. Now. Us. You know what I mean. I don't like feeling distant from you."

I shift positions and sand runs into my left shoe.

I know exactly what she means. Especially since I'll squirm under Malcolm's thumb again tomorrow. Absently, she rubs the side of her head. A migraine coming on, one stronger than the psilocybin microdose. I've become a headache for her while she has become my solace. I can't cancel the second interview. I need her to ask me questions, need her to help me see again. The breakers roll in fast and hard, spraying white foam off their crests. Staring at the ocean, she says:

"The waves are unwaving."

CHAPTER NINETEEN

"A gang of robbers in hiding," Malcolm says. "They act like Robin Hood and his merry mobsters, or the Bolsheviks looting banks to finance the revolution, but they're nothing more than modern day robber barons."

"You're talking about the Dijkstra Foundation again?" I reply. "They don't seem to hide much at all. They hang a shiny plaque on what they own."

"The glow of European respectability as camouflage. The bright cloak that obscures their greedy filth."

We sit overlooking the ocean again, Malcolm in his wheelchair, me on my flat granite altar. He is dressed in a brown Bottega Veneta robe and, no sunglasses today, looks drugged to his dark eyeballs. I am strangely calm, knowing it's the last time we will meet. I considered not coming at all, just texting him a farewell message. But I've preached "closure" to my clients for two decades, so here I am in the final act.

I expected some new shock in this session, expected him to cut my pay again, or reveal new photos of compromising positions, something that would emphatically ignite my farewell, but he is rambling on the verge of incoherence. Maybe he really is drugged senseless. Yet even if his manner is loose and distracted, his gaze still calculates. I think he knows I'm about to leave him, so he brandishes absurdity to keep me guessing. He speaks of "disharmonic social privilege" and "an unbalanced society with its rigid stratification into classes." Soon he'll shift gears and bring up the Code of Ethics, his shark lawyer, Beth's contract with the Dijkstra Foundation. It doesn't matter. I'm gone.

He looks down at his hands, scratches the back of his left hand. He slides off into further digression, says his oncologist and dermatologist agree that his heavy opioid cocktail may cause "dilatation of cutaneous blood vessels." Thus, periodic itching. He speculates, "It might be the buprenorphine I take."

Or the amphetamines, I think.

"It stops the pain," he adds, "but brings ocean fog into my skull, makes me drowsy."

I glance out at the waves, at the soupy cloud floating in over the surge and swell. It doesn't have to enter his head, I think. It already resembles gray matter.

"However," he goes on, staring at his hand as if searching for dilated vessels himself, "I was clear about one thing from the very start. I knew that you and my wife would be hog-wild for each other."

I sit forward an inch on the altar. In a minute he'll begin talking about Beth's thighs again. He's lighting the fuse to ignite my farewell.

"It's why I showed her your YouTube videos," he goes on. "Your opera house act at Esalen. I knew it would perk her up. Such a sensitive, caring man, so wise in the ways of couples which, with her romantic nose always stuffed into poetry, she has never had much luck."

He will die, I think, very soon this will end. Whether or not I vanish this minute or the next, the farewell is ordained.

"And, of course, she is put together nicely in physical terms," he says, "her thighs and whatnot, as we've already discussed, man to man, so to speak. But I knew the quiet dazzle of her education would be what really turned your tap on full flow. Yale and the Sorbonne, belles-lettres and languages, her very own literary rag. Very sexy stuff. Opposites attract and all that twin soul twaddle."

"Beth says you didn't marry her," I tell him. "You married her name, her imagined property. She says you were so busy feigning a lack of interest in the Dijkstra Foundation to fool her that you ended up fooling yourself."

Beth never said any such thing. Maybe she thought it countless times but those words never reached my ears. I'm fed up and furious, that's all. The majestic coastal slope of the Santa Lucia range and the sublime Pacific reproach my false words.

"That doesn't sound like something my wife would say," Malcolm replies. "Regardless, I planted a seed..."

Now is the moment to do my vanishing act, but I want to know what he's talking about. A bolt of pain shakes his torso. He winces, grips the joystick as if literally hanging on to dear life. Slowly, he brings himself under control.

"You were telling me about a seed..." I say.

"Yes, I planted one. I arranged for you and her to meet alone. That's all it took. A couple of innocent meetings. So much allure in so short a time. Now her European empire foundation which is rightly owed me is within reach." His voice hardens. "So no more suspense. Speak up. Did you find the damn contract or not?"

As I rise to my feet, a gust of fresh air washes across my face. "I've had enough, Malcolm," I say firmly. "You can do whatever you want. I'm out of here. Goodbye and good luck with your European treasure hunt."

He gives a laugh, more like a snort. "Let's read something first." He reaches into his robe. "It's only the first paragraph of a rough draft but it'll tickle your therapeutic fancy."

I start to turn away but his perverse confidence warns me that he's planting another seed. He taps the joystick, clears his throat theatrically. "Ahem." He reads in a monotone:

"'I have struggled to survive this cruel moment but in the end I can't bear any more ruthless humiliation and relentless pain. I hoped that Ryan Mathiesson would save my marriage and then I prayed he would save me, but first he ravaged my wife and then he set about destroying me. In the guise of a therapist, he feeds on weakness, enjoys sadistic pleasure. He and my wife tortured me further by publicly ridiculing my marriage in a series of twisted interviews.'"

He looks up, smiles. "I suppose it's a touch overwrought with all these 'R' words. Ruthless. Relentless. Ravage. And, of course, the 'twisted interviews' is open to interpretation, but it gets the point across. I may add a line or two about you and my wife torturing me further by using my failed marriage as fodder for your professional ambitions. Something like that."

"Whatever you write," I reply, "you can be sure *The Coast Quarterly* won't print it."

He laughs. "I suppose not, but the *Monterey Herald* might and your comrades at the Counseling Center will read it with gusto. I know it will make great entertainment as a podcast, so I'll record it as well. But why do you say 'Whatever you write'? Surely, as a therapist, you must recognize the first paragraph of a suicide note."

"What?" Involuntarily, I take a step backward and my heel hits the boulder.

"I'm going to die anyway. So why not have some fun on my way out? If I can't get what I want, why should you run off scot free? I've given death-bed instructions to my lawyer to raise havoc with all this after I'm gone. Use your imagination and you'll get a good idea of what she'll do. Be quick in giving your second interview because *The Coast Quarterly* won't be around for a third."

I tremble in front of him. What truly horrifies me isn't his malice or even the havoc his shark lawyer will wreak. It's knowing he will enjoy committing suicide.

"Find the damn contract," he commands, "and bring it to me."

CHAPTER TWENTY

*O*ur special marriage-themed issue of The Coast Quarterly *now presents the second part of our three-part interview featuring marriage therapist Ryan Mathiesson. With twenty years of experience counseling troubled couples, Ryan Mathiesson has been a frequent contributor to popular internet forums as well as to his own highly visited web page, The Marriage Dance. On yet another foggy day, he once again sits down with Founding Editor Elizabeth Dijkstra in our Carmel office, this time to discuss The Metaphysics of Marriage. As always, the podcast of this exchange is freely available to subscribers at* The Coast Quarterly *webpage.*

ED: When we left off, you said that we all seek a twin soul. It seems a good place to begin our talk on *The Metaphysics of Marriage*. A great deal has recently been written on the concept of the twin soul.

RM: Most of it garbage. A valentine mentality which cheapens and trivializes while pretending to glorify. The idea that we may meet a soul mate who will make our life and very existence complete is not only false, but dangerous.

ED: Yet you maintain that we innately set out on the search for our twin soul.

RM: It doesn't mean we have to revere passion and

romance at the expense of serenity and inner peace. The search is the thing. The yearning.

ED: But why yearn if not to—

RM: The yearning is wired into our genes. It not only sparks the search, but keeps it alive. To keep us alive. *Alive* in the sense of awake, alert, conscious. Our quest for the twin flame is a universal desire etched onto our souls. We seek pure love and numinous union in a polar opposite. If we are blessed and this desire manifests as part of our destiny, we render the moment sacred by performing a sacrament called marriage. Some type of wedding ceremony has existed in every known human society since ancient times.

ED: So far so good. What's the problem?

RM: We now live in an age in which poetically minded couples write their own vows. Friends, 'internet experts' and wedding planners preside over our marriage ceremonies. To our great misfortune, a wedding has become a mere cultural event, and a cheap one at that, a chance to dress up in pretty clothes and snap selfies at a party. Once sacred vows dictated by a higher power have become self-authored gibberish. In essence, bride and groom declare: 'I can no longer stand being alone, so I hereby chain my soul to another and call it lifelong commitment."

ED: I repeat that you sound pessimistic. You depict marriage as Act One in a short theatrical play titled Divorce. Can't we say that two souls meet and marry because they strive to become more than they are, greater than they are?

RM: Not if they meet in a no-man's land of rapture and illusion, courting each other and disaster at the same time. Beginning at such soaring heights, where can any marriage go but down? How long before hearts burst and nuptial blood flows? Sadly, we are addicted. Our souls ache and we crave romance—demand romance—so we throw ourselves into desperate dreams of a perfect lover, a twin flame.

ED: You're the one who says we're on a quest for—

RM: Our perfect lover. Yes, and one day we may meet him or her. But not until we're ready. So we can't waste any more time. We have to make ourselves ready.

ED: And how do we do that?

RM: We can start by consuming less of the swill Hollywood feeds us. At least we don't have to digest it so seriously. At some point we have to question ourselves.

ED: Certainly a few films can't be held responsible for all our marital ills.

RM: A few? More like thousands over the course of fifty, sixty, seventy years. All of that doesn't go into your psyche like popcorn into your stomach. It stays there and breeds. It filters into the subconscious, clouds perception, creates illusions. This isn't some vague opinion or theory I have in my head, some funny, weird idea. It's the hardcore truth I see every day of the week, month after month, year after year. The movie ends in my consultation office. Rapture turns into despair, euphoria becomes pointless existence, ideal love nothing but a withered fantasy. Broken men and women cry their tormented hearts out. If you witness this day in and day out as I do, you can only reach one conclusion. Our concept of love is deeply flawed.

ED: *(hesitates)* Rilke said that the highest form of love is to be the protector of another person's solitude.

RM: Okay, then we might ask ourselves, "If I meet my perfect lover, how might I best protect his or her solitude?"

ED: I repeat: how do we do that?

RM: The deeper the solitude, the greater the love. So we start by protecting our own solitude. If we don't know how to do it for ourselves, we're sure to bungle it with somebody else.

ED: At heart, you're implying that we don't know how to be alone.

RM: We get *lonely*. Then depressed. It's one of the reasons we're so desperate to meet a perfect lover. To save ourselves from depression, loneliness, existential dread.

ED: Rilke also wrote of Orpheus and Eurydice, a love story which contains more than a little Hollywood passion.

RM: Orpheus searches for his perfect lover in the land of the dead, among shadows, much as we wander through dark bars and discotheques in search of someone who will transport us into the land of the living. Our literature of famous lovers usually involves the death of one or both lovers. Tristan and Isolde, Madame Bovary, Echo and Narcissus, Romeo and that other person.

ED: What does this tell us?

RM: There is always the danger that our intense longing and quest for the twin flame may mistakenly and tragically devolve into drama. In her letters to Abelard, Heloise wrote: "True tenderness makes us separate the lover from all that is external to him..." She was speaking about the tenderness of the soul. How many of us are even in contact with it, let alone capable of separating our lover from his or her wealth, looks, social position and the drama of our desire?

ED: Rather than a marriage therapist, you sound like a wedding sentinel guarding the altar.

RM: If I were, I would interrupt the sacred vows and say: "Think now before you utter another word. Think very carefully. Your well-being and peace of mind are at stake."

ED: Would anyone listen?

RM: Even if they did, they probably wouldn't hear. None of us arrive at the altar seeking such an earful. But two souls desperate to fuse can only become confused. At least we might consider that we could be wrong from the start. We plant ourselves in the garden of sacred union. Two separate selves planted separately, allowing room to grow, to take root in nutritious soil, to absorb water and sunlight. How long before one begins to cast shadow onto the other?

ED: What does metaphysical literature have to say about marriage?

RM: Carl Jung wrote of the *mysterium coniunctionis,* the mystery of unification. He said that *hieragamos,* or divine union, was attained out of a need for psychic harmony and equilibrium, the balancing of the tension of polar opposites. King and queen, man and woman, sun and moon, light and darkness, yin and yang—in these relationships we have the possibility to transmute chaos into synergy. Coming together in the *mysterium coniunctionis,* we dance with our partner in hostility and ill will or twirl together in ardor and intimacy.

ED: Are we speaking of Jung's ideas now or yours?

RM: I might be putting some of my words into Jung's mouth.

ED: Then let's hear your own. When you refer to the 'metaphysics of marriage,' what do you mean? What exactly is the 'marriage dance?'

RM: It is man, woman and emptiness.

ED: Emptiness?

RM: The silence, the space between the notes that make the music. The crack in the door through which moonlight enters. The empty space between the dancers. Without emptiness, there is no music, light or dance.

ED: A moment ago I said you sounded like a sentinel guarding the altar. Yet sometimes when you speak, you seem to evoke the power of ancestral tradition, like a rabbi performing his duties.

RM: Age-old rituals and religious patterns channel the collective Unconscious. They are inherited wisdom and they exist for a reason. If you simply want to put a ring on a finger, go on a honeymoon and have some children, okay, good luck and have fun. But we are speaking of the poetry of alchemical love, the metaphysics of marriage. In other words, long before we stand on quicksand at the high altar, we need to lower ourselves and bow to a greater power. Our vows must be made for us—inherited by us—before we ourselves declare any eternal promise. Only then may we and our perfect lover unite.

Chapter Twenty-one

I feel like I should take back half my words and correct them, change their tone. I don't know where they came from. Once again, I didn't sound like myself. It's as if I put on a formal, academic guise for the interview. The educated gentleman. The almost scholar. Did I fabricate all of that about Jung? I must have because I've never been able to read the guy. I always found him too dense, too complicated, too brilliant. Then I go and sound like he's my best friend.

"Thanks, Bernie," Beth says. "Just make sure you back it up."

Bernie nods, packs up the mikes and shields, fusses with his laptop. When he leaves, Beth leans onto her desk and jots down a note. I watch her hair fall forward off her shoulder. Strange, but it's no longer dishwater blond. It's changed to ash, streaks of light gray underneath. How did that happen? Living cooped up in this book-lined cottage instead of her airy palace. The psilocybin microdose. Going through divorce hell with Malcolm. It has depleted her, smothered her innate vitality. Or maybe I'm the one who feels depleted, once again eviscerated by her damn interview.

"Time for a drink?" she asks.

"Sure." This is my chance, I think. I can decide later if I use it.

She smiles and asks if I'd like to go anywhere special. I hesitate. Where I should go is down to the beach. I should stand before the vast matrix of the sea and drink in healthy gulps of Mother Nature. But I shrug and ask if she'd mind going out for a bottle of something while I "put myself back together." Apt expression. As if I've come apart at the seams. From noble to *unnoble* in less than an hour.

She makes a joke about manning the fort and leaves. I sit dead still. The office grows silent and I can hear—or think I can hear—the nearby ocean. I've made a mistake. If I stay here, I'm obliged to search. I should be with the Sunday crowd enjoying the beach, attuning myself to oceanic rhythms.

Instead, I rise to my feet and move quickly to the window. I pull the curtains closed. If anyone is filming today, let them film that. Then I hurry to Beth's desk. The large center drawer opens easily. So do two of the smaller side drawers. The bottom side drawer is locked tight. I rifle through the messy contents of the center drawer and soon find a plastic bowl which holds assorted paper clips, rubber bands and a silver key. I glance at the curtained window and open the bottom drawer, demanding of myself: What am I doing? Am I protecting my lover's solitude?

The drawer opens. It is full of files and papers. A birth certificate, car insurance, health insurance, several pages bearing a Yale letterhead, an Enneagram test, some kind of an award or acknowledgement in French, three weathered journals and a folder marked "Dijkstra Foundation." I throw another look at the curtains and open the folder. There are several signed contracts but one in particular catches my eye. Three pages of legalese entitled "Pacific House Agreement." I feel sick to my stomach but think, "Do it now. Decide later."

The loud ring of the desk phone makes my heart jump. I stare at the thing in horror, as if it somehow knows what I'm doing. Should I answer it? I decide not to. But it forces me to take my cell phone from my pocket. I turned it off before the interview. Now I turn it back on and find messages from Beth. Quickly, I snap a half dozen photos of the contract and return it to the drawer, making sure the pile of folders remains in order. I lock the drawer, put the key back in the plastic bowl, close the center drawer and double check everything. It looks good but the desk phone has been ringing all this time, jangling my nerves. I grab the receiver and in my best secretarial tone say, *"Coast Quarterly,* can I help you?"

"Are you taking a nap or what?" Beth says.

"I— guess I did doze off," I mumble. My morals took forty winks. "What's up?"

She says she tried to call my cell and I tell her that I forgot to turn it back on. My voice sounds normal, maybe somewhat forced. She says she is in a liquor store and there is a sale on wine from "a good bodega." She has been wavering over "a nice Cab or a Sauvignon Blanc." Which would I prefer? "Let's go red," I reply smoothly.

I hang up and scurry to the window, open the curtains. Then I return to the chair I occupied when Beth walked out the door, entrusting me with her office. I look at my phone and discover a message from Malcolm. *Have you found anything?* Christ, does he know my thoughts in the moment I think them? I shove the phone into my pocket and struggle to find a casual sitting position. As before, it seems I can hear the ocean's roar but it's my heart banging against my chest. A minute ago I asked myself what I was doing. Now I interrogate a stranger, demanding to know what I've just done.

I achieve a position which seems nonchalant, hang loose, like I have just awoken from another nap. Everything will be okay, I think. I may have the information Malcolm wants but it doesn't mean I have to give it to him. Even if I hand it over, what can he do? Whether the contract proclaims Beth as the renter, owner or temporary resident of Pacific House, the Dijkstra Foundation's international legal team would never draw up an agreement a vindictive husband could breach. The shark lawyer will have nothing to chew on. It's Malcolm's frustrated attempt to control what's beyond his control, that's all. His wife of one month left him and he lost the mansion he married her for. Besides everything else, he'll be dead long before a divorce is finalized, let alone an imagined property settlement with the Dijkstra Foundation.

Beth arrives with the Cab and some aged cheddar. She hands me the bottle and a corkscrew and begins to cut the cheese into nibble-sized chunks. She glances at me.

"Are you hot?" she asks.

"Hot?"

"You're sweating."

I put a hand to my forehead. "You're right." I take out my handkerchief, mop my brow. "Probably still hot under the collar after your grill session."

She smiles vaguely, says, "Anyway, let's have a drink and head down to the beach. Get some fresh air."

She serves the cheese and I pour wine. We talk about the interview. She thinks it went well, maybe even better than the first one. She says she is never really sure until she sees it all in print and can do some editing. That makes sense, I reply. My voice still sounds forced. I have to stop sweating, I tell myself. I'm beginning to feel seriously ill, not just my stomach, more like I've walked out of a bright, sunny room and stumbled down broken stairs into a dank cellar.

Beth seems not to notice my discomfort. She goes on talking. She says that our referring to Rilke during the interview reminded her of something he wrote. She's been trying to think of it since stepping out to the liquor store but can't bring it to mind. She walks over to the shelves, scans titles, selects a book, flips through pages.

"Here it is." She reads to herself, sips wine, and then reads out loud with feeling:

"'For one human being to love another is perhaps the

most difficult of all tasks, the ultimate and final test for which all other work is mere preparation.'"

"That's quite the statement," I say, and immediately regret it. Calling the quote a "statement" not only trivializes my lover's emotions, but demeans the grandeur of Rilke's thought, his far-echoing truth.

But Beth's thoughts are also far off. I'm not sure she even heard me. Ruefully, she says: "I'd like to say Malcolm was my 'ultimate and final test,' but I suppose I'm still preparing."

"He's obsessed," I reply without thinking. My second regret. I told her I wouldn't speak of him. It's his text message, that and my guilt for violating the contents of her desk.

"It's been a tendency for most of my adult life," she replies.

"Tendency?"

"To get involved with men who are obsessed."

I feel a door open wide with implication. "Well, now you're involved with me," I say, opening the door wider yet.

She nods, reaches for a square of cheese.

I press her. "Okay, I'll bite—what's my obsession?"

She doesn't even have to think about it. I might have asked her the color of my eyes.

"You ask like you don't know," she says. She waits for me to give a response and when I don't, she says: "You're obsessed with finding your perfect lover, your soul mate, your twin flame."

I pinch the stem of my wine glass. "Well, I'm certainly interested in the theme..."

"The *theme* has propelled you through your life," she says, munching on the cheese. "You told me you began in your teen years, impelled by your parents' vile marriage. Now here you are giving an interview on the theme. Tell the truth. Don't you think of me as your twin flame?"

What I think is that this conversation is strange and going nowhere. Why did she say *Tell the truth?* Does she somehow sense my violating her privacy? The fear that I might lose her shakes me. I relent, cast aside defenses.

"What I know," I say sincerely, "is that my feelings for you contain all the heat of a twin flame, beginning with a burning sense of destiny, of fated encounter."

That stops her. "Oh," she says, "you should have mentioned that in the interview."

"We're not doing an interview now. We're talking. Two lovers talking."

"It's beginning to sound more like two lovers arguing. Arguing stupidly."

"Then let's be smart," I say, "and drop it."

We put away the wine and cheese and wander our way down to the beach. We find what I imagined earlier: a Sunday crowd enjoying the ocean like a vast refreshment. I can feel people releasing tension, becoming revitalized. Dynamic Mother Nature. Unlimited, unconfined by boundaries.

"I'm still thinking about what you said," Beth says. "About destiny and fated encounter. We'll have to bring it up in the third interview. Do you know the etymology of the word *desire?*"

"No idea." Right now I don't even know what etymology is.

"It means to await what the stars will bring."

I regard her with surprise and a thrill of recognition: she is my lover and she is wonderful. I tell her: "That sounds more like a description of *destiny.*"

"It's what I think too."

I force myself to look away from her. I recall what I said earlier about Orpheus and Eurydice. I have no lyre and wouldn't know how to play one if I did, but I too would chase this woman into the Underworld. Chase her deep into the Underworld and bring her all the way out. Don't look back, Ryan.

The beach begins to fill, people arriving for the sunset. Some unfurl blankets and colorful towels. An elderly woman in a battered straw hat sets up a small lawn chair near us. She catches me observing her, smiles warmly and says, "It's the best place on earth to watch a sunset." Hard to argue with that. Loose strings of horizon clouds light up in yellow and burnt orange. The sun sends blazing streaks of gold across the waves, into Beth's hair, setting the ash aglow. So no argument about the beauty, but I still feel sick to my stomach. I look up and down the shoreline, then turn and look behind us. Our two shadows are stretched out across the sand, close but still separate.

CHAPTER TWENTY-TWO

Our shadows on the white sand impart no sensation of romance. Rather, they remind me that we are being shadowed. Even if nothing salacious can be filmed, Malcolm still has eyes on us. I check my cell, tilting the screen away from Beth, and discover a new message from him. *I said, did you find anything?* Now the words are phrased as if he knows we are out of the office. I glance around, doubly sure we are being forked over in real time. Beth picks up on my unease, but misreads it.

"Are you worried about something?" she asks. "The interview? A client?"

"You can't take clients home with you," I answer professionally. "It's Rule Number One. Or maybe Number Two. Preserve psychic distance."

"As in their problems aren't your problems?"

"That and it's another way of saying that no matter how horrifying the chaos, in the end they have to face it themselves."

She nods, thoughtful. "Still, it must be hard at times..."

"Many times." Especially when I take Malcolm everywhere with me. Home, the supermarket, the office, and now the beach.

The sun sinks, carrying our white sand shadows into ocean depths. Across the beach people rise to their feet, collect their things, call their dogs. We join the twilight exodus.

"Speaking of clients," I say, "I want to ask you about Malcolm."

Her head swivels but we are now side by side and on the move so she can't look directly into my eyes.

"I thought that topic was off limits," she says.

"It was," I reply, "and should be. But talking about psychic distance... I feel like I've painted myself into a corner. Time is short and I need to find answers."

"Answers to what?"

"I need to know who he is."

"Good luck with that."

"Could you be a little more specific?"

"He is whoever he wants to be according to what he can get out of you. You can be sure you haven't painted yourself into a corner. He's painted you there, maneuvered you into a spot so tight your shoulders ache..."

I can't see her eyes either, but her tone contains a note of cruelty that surprises me. We pass a few cottages, come to a cafe terrace, choose a table, order two lattes. In a gentler voice, she says, "Speaking of painting... there's one in my study in Pacific House entitled 'Solicitude.' It's by an unknown artist and of no real value except that I've had it since childhood. I can actually remember gazing up at it from my crib."

"What's it's of?" I sense her trying to change the subject.

"A child giving birds a drink at a fountain. My family

moved a lot, back and forth between Virginia and southern France, Boston and Den Hague, but no matter where we lived, the painting always hung on the wall above my bed."

The lattes arrive. I stir mine, thinking of my own childhood. Europe could have been in Antarctica for all I knew. Beth goes on to say that as a young girl, she thought Solicitude was the unknown artist's name. With maturity, she came to understand the word as describing an eagerness to "quench the thirst of less-evolved beings." She believed the connection between "child" and "birds" implied an intuitive rapport, a soul-touch at the level of pure feeling. I nod but now I'm certain she's trying to change the subject.

"What you receive from the Infinite," she adds, "you can give to finite beings who thirst for it. You might even say that somewhere in my depths, the painting provided the inspiration for *The Coast Quarterly*."

"Because it's like a fountain of learning?"

"Because it allows me to give back some of what I've been given."

"It's a lovely thought," I say, "but I don't see what it has to do with Malcolm."

"You asked who he is. I'm trying to tell you. The first time he saw the painting was the first time I caught an inkling of something not right. A below-ground tremor. An off-beat pulse. Somehow I sensed that behind his affable, charming expression of curiosity and interest there was an ugly sneer."

"The painting seemed corny to him?"

"I'd guess it seemed banal, sappy, laughable. He'd probably like to take the water away from the birds, or plug up the fountain."

I abstain from another sip of latte. Again, her bitterness surprises me, but I have to admit the subject didn't change.

"And I married him," she goes on with less rancor but more regret. "A worldly wise woman of thirty-five and I acted like one of the birds at the fountain. I chirped and offered him my innocence."

Someone drops a plate onto a nearby table, turning both our heads. I take a moment to scan other tables. I lower my voice.

"When you agreed to come to couple therapy," I ask, "was it because you thought you could wash your hands of him, turn him over to me and hotfoot it out of a bad marriage?"

She stares at her latte, seems to speak to it. "I'm ashamed to say it's exactly what I thought. It's also the only thing that surprised him. He calculated everything else five steps and five days ahead of me, but I moved out of Pacific House on impulse and it caught him off guard. Or so I think. Who knows?" She looks up from the latte. "Could we talk about something else, please? I liked it better when this was off limits."

"Just one more thing. Did you ever visit any of his buildings or construction projects?"

She bites down on a wry grin. "Malcolm the architect? I never even saw a sketch. He had books he was apparently reading. Studies on construction technique and vernacular design that he could have picked up at any used bookstore. Occasionally he disappeared for a couple of days to visit a 'site in southern Texas' or a 'proposed location outside Phoenix.'"

"But he made money somewhere."

"Bundles. Maybe a former wife, maybe drugs, maybe embezzlement or some Ponzi scheme. He convinced me he had no interest in money, no interest in Pacific House except from a professional point of view."

We fall quiet. She drinks the rest of her latte, sets her cup onto its matching saucer. She seems content to remain silent but then changes her mind.

"I refused to believe it," she says with feeling. "Refused to believe that anyone could be so poisonous, so I chastised myself for my own evil thoughts. That was my problem, my birdlike innocence. Then along came terminal illness. I read the oncologist's report trembling in guilt and dismay. Maybe you feel something similar. Maybe you believe every client has some good in them and it's just a matter of finding it."

She's right, but I'm loath to admit what reveals me as deficient, less than the all-knowing therapist she has just interviewed. I lean forward on the table.

"You just said it," I murmur. "The show is about to end and he knows it. It's easy to be offended by him, angered by his aggression and manipulation, but you haven't seen him lately. He's in a wheelchair. On morphine. Disintegrating. One foot already in hell. An omnipotent force greater than any pride or demon is approaching. No power on earth can stand in its way and he knows it."

"If you think or hope there might be some deathbed conversion," she says slowly, "you couldn't be more wrong. No matter the pain, no matter the darkness, he won't recant and he sure won't plead for some last rite."

I shake my head. "Nobody consciously dives into eternal damnation."

"He will. With his last breath. Be certain. Don't become so hung up with saving him that you doom yourself. He'll do everything he can to drag you down with him."

I sit back, nudge the handle of my coffee cup with my forefinger. Much of what she has just said isn't so different from when she described Malcolm's many masks. But I didn't know her then, hadn't yet made love with her and held her in my arms. Nor had I yet lied to her. Now, head throbbing, I feel both her pain and my deceit. She is still trapped by what I call Malcolm's iron will, by what she terms his malevolence. Not a bird at a fountain but one in a cage. I glance around the cafe terrace like he's here with us. And, of course, he is. If I'm here, so is he.

***

Warmth on my thoracic vertebrae stirs me awake. I linger on a last thread of sleep before becoming aware that Beth lies behind me. Her forehead rests on the nape of my neck and her partially opened mouth rests against my spinal cord. I never realized that someone's breath could pass through flesh into another person's body. The warmth enters me, radiating onto my vertebrae, then outward as far as my shoulder blades. I awaken further, grow more conscious of her warmth. If I have a twin soul, it may be in that breath, in the hub of that radiance. Her right arm rests atop my ribs, her legs scrunched up into the backs of my thighs, my calves. We are in my house, my bed. The first time we have made love in a bed, not on a sofa in her office. We are curled up together in an embryo, the ancient moan of the sea lions in the night.

Gently, I lift her arm and slip out of her embrace. I roll off the bed, locate my robe. I take my cell phone off the nightstand and pad noiselessly across the room. Out in the hall, I pull the door closed behind me. Waving my arm in front of me, I walk down the hall to the kitchen and stand by the sink. Looking out into the back garden, I feel Beth's breath vanishing from inside me. I must do something, I think. I must protect her warmth, her solitude.

But I can't bring myself to turn on my phone and look at the Pacific House contract. It doesn't matter if the photos prove that Malcolm is wrong. I never should have taken them in the first place. But it's too late to scold myself. Likewise, too late to confess my crime to Beth. As I well know from twenty years on the job, betrayal destroys relationships and mine has joined me to my lover's maniacal ex. To imagine telling her is to envision her face twisted in disgust. Everything she said about Malcolm on the beach or at the cafe would become what she can say about me. Her final words, since I would never see her again.

The only other option is to keep the photos hidden from Malcolm and pray he doesn't make good on his threat of suicide—or pray that he dies before making good on it. I fear that Beth will discover my treachery. Fear that I will be disgraced at the Counseling Center, ruined by a lawsuit. But they are recent fears and my greatest fear has been with me for decades: a client committing suicide. Somehow Malcolm must have sensed it. It's the gun he holds at my head, the one that forced me to take the photos in the first place.

I consider delaying things by telling him my phone is in the repair shop, that it's going to take a while for the technician to retrieve all the images. But nobody would believe it, let alone Malcolm, and text messages are probably piling up right this minute. *Did you find anything? I want to see the contract now.* Beth said it in plain English: he'll delight in dragging me down. Even if he has to blow his own brains out to do it.

I look past my reflection in the window. In the semi-darkness, a light fog enshrouds the garden. Wisps of mist float above the rose bushes. I turn on the faucet and run water into a glass. I take a sip. The sea lions drone on down at Fisherman's Wharf. Strange night.

A movement in the darkness near the neighbor's garage catches my eye. In the following moment, a blacktail deer steps into view and sets about browsing the bushes. I look at the fog beyond the garage. When one deer appears, Jenny told me, two or three others usually follow.

Tingles run up my spine, chasing off the last of Beth's breath. A ghost, I think. Blended into the mist, moving slowly, a pure white stag, as white as the winter fog, steps forward into the roses. I can just distinguish its white throat and flanks, its pink ears and nose, a gleam of fugitive moonlight on its antlers. Goose bumps run along my arms and then the creature is gone, trotting off into the fog. I rattle the glass setting it back down on the counter. The sea lions go on barking. I recall the story Malcolm told me about his childhood hunting initiation, the young boy tied to a tree, the disemboweled deer carcass over his head. I must do something, I think again.

I turn on my cell phone and scroll through the photos of the "Pacific House Agreement." I shouldn't be doing this in the middle of the night. The legalese is thick and my sleepy mind is slow. I come to a set of clauses, which I read twice. Their meaning is evident but I still read them again. Clearly and beyond doubt, the contract states that Beth is the undisputed owner of Pacific House as well as *The Coast Quarterly* cottage, a house in Den Hague and an apartment in Paris. I look out at the garden, now covered in the winter mist. It seems betrayal is a two-way street.

CHAPTER TWENTY-THREE

I park the car on the edge of the woods a hundred yards from the gated entrance. Pacific House is just visible in the distance, the ocean a blur farther beyond. Still twenty minutes before my session with Malcolm. I switch on my cell phone and reread the "Pacific House Agreement." Nothing has changed since last night in the kitchen. A couple of minor clauses state that various paintings, statuary and objets d'art contained in Pacific House belong to the Dijkstra Foundation. The Foundation may use Pacific House on occasion "as a temporary exhibition space for the display of fine artworks," but only upon receiving prior written permission from Beth. She is clearly the owner, clearly a liar.

I am tempted to turn the car around and drive back into Monterey, pack up my belongings and head down Highway One straight into my lost life in LA. Or into some other life where I am no longer a naive therapist deluded and beguiled by a moribund psychopath and his mendacious wife.

I wonder what would have happened if I had insisted from the start—as I should have—to see them together as a couple whether for a troubled marriage or an impending death. How long would the sessions have lasted? A week, two weeks, three before they traipsed off to play games elsewhere. But, no, I wanted to change my life and help a fellow human being in agony. That's what I said. Or did I take on a new client as a direct path to his gorgeous wife? His wife who wanted to wash her hands of him and hired me to do the washing.

I stare through the windshield at the estate grounds. What is it about Pacific House that I cannot see? I recall what Malcolm asked me. *Can you even imagine what this property is worth?* The question still disgusts me. Yet now I can imagine *The Coast Quarterly* adding a footnote to my interview: overmatched therapist burns out on twin-flame dreams.

I have to pull myself together. I can confront Beth later; right now I have Malcolm to deal with. The cliff edge and granite altar stone are beyond my field of vision. I can't determine if our session will take place by the sea or inside Pacific House, perhaps in a room near the painting of a child with birds at a fountain. Solicitude. Does it exist or is it just another tale told in the tangled web?

The sun begins its descent into murky blue waves. Still a full dark night before a rooster's cry heralds a new sunrise. The cock crows at dawn to give voice to what is unmanifested. The cry should be a creative and joyous response but I am the rooster who thinks he makes the sun ascend. That's what has blinded me, the dazzle I created. Fake dazzle. Now, facing Malcolm, I need to set the eastern horizon on fire.

I start the engine, drive through the main gate and

enter Pacific House grounds. Yetta, rigid, silent, terrified that I might ask a question, guides me past the library, the billiard room, the kitchen. I walk out onto the rolling yard. No Mexican gardener today. At the cliff edge Malcolm waits in his wheelchair. He is hunched forward, weakened, wrapped in a brown blanket. His eyes stare at me, insistent, as I take my seat on the granite altar stone.

"You didn't reply to my messages," he says. A simple phrase but he pronounces it like a judge about to pass sentence on a fractious prisoner.

"I wanted to tell you in person."

"Tell me then."

"Beth went out to the store and left me alone in the office. There's a locked drawer in her desk but I managed to find the key. It was buried in a bowl of paper clips and erasers."

"Yes, so what? Go on."

"I'm trying to tell you that it took time, a lot of time. But I finally found the key, opened the drawer and came upon a pile of folders. Insurance papers and certificates. The contract was there."

He sits forward in the wheelchair, squeezing the joystick in his left hand. I maintain a tranquil pose but wonder if I'm truly setting the horizon on fire or just lighting another blaze beneath my own feet.

"It's three pages long," I go on, "entitled Pacific House Agreement. I reached for my cell phone but then

I checked the window and saw Beth crossing the street. I didn't have time to photograph the contract. I barely got everything put back before she walked in."

He regards me searchingly. I resist saying anything more. Embellishment will only adorn me in suspicion. He looks aside, thinking. I experience momentary dizziness. The sun quivers above the ocean as if stationing retrograde. Waves pound the rock face at the base of the cliff. Malcolm looks back at me.

"I don't believe you," he says. "What did you read in the contract?"

"I just told you. No time to read or photograph anything."

"But you opened the drawer, looked through papers, found the contract?"

"What did I just say? Are you listening to me?"

"Very closely. As if I were your therapist."

"Funny." I have the impression he is so intimate with lies and deceit he instantly recognizes them in others. "The point is, it just didn't work."

"The point," he says slowly, "is that you will make it work. You can *curtain* off the outer world but not the inner."

"What?"

"State-of-the-art security is a salient and ubiquitous feature of the Dijkstra Foundation. Witness the cameras around Pacific House. They film every insect crawling on a window, every crumb falling off a table. We are being filmed as we sit here. To my knowledge, there are at least two security cameras inside *The Coast Quarterly* office. If you rummaged through the drawer as you say—the part of your story I believe—then the act has been recorded for posterity. And for my wife. Imagine how wide her pretty eyes will open."

My voice cracks. "I— I didn't steal anything."

He laughs. "If you tried, you couldn't sound more pathetic. But you needn't worry. At least not right now. Dijkstra Foundation Security only reviews taped footage when they have probable cause. A broken window, a jimmied lock. If you didn't steal anything, then they have no reason to look at their footage."

Reflexively, I insist. "Of course I didn't steal anything."

He laughs again, pleased that I have snatched up his bait. I glance at the sun. It has stopped moving. Did I really envision a new dawn?

"Then the only remaining danger is the possibility of a tip," Malcolm says, observing my anxious look with pleasure. "An anonymous tip. A concerned citizen calling to report suspicious activity on such and such a date. It could happen any time the citizen decides to act." He coughs, gasps for breath. "Then, of course, Dijkstra Foundation Security would be obliged to review footage. Meanwhile, before the call is made, I strongly suggest you get me the information on this Pacific House Agreement."

His threat is dressed in an expression of false

pleasantness. A mask I haven't yet seen. But he has managed to re-create the film and set it running in my head. From a fish-eye, ceiling-level view, I observe myself closing the curtain, rifling through drawers, jumping out of my pants at the jangling phone, snapping the photos, opening the curtain, racing back to my chair. The film ends with Beth arriving, cutting up cheese and asking, "Don't you think of me as being your twin flame?"

My heart hammers. I force out a controlled phrase. "Malcolm, listen to me. You're dying. You're the one who told me, so you must know it. But you speak and act like your day will never end, like you have countless hours to clown around being devious."

It seems my words have hit home, broken through the barrier of his manic disregard. Then his eyes darken, his left hand jiggles the joystick and the wheelchair swivels a few inches to the left. "Yes, I'm dying," he replies without feeling. "Very kind of you to remind me. Now let me remind you of something. Anyone about to leave the world wants to put their affairs in order. I am no different. In the short time I have remaining, I will do everything possible to attain that end. And you will help me. What belongs to me, will belong to me. Be sure of that. Even if my lawyer must prove it in court as I watch from the grave."

Once again, the strain of saying so much causes him to lose breath. He inhales deeply, raggedly. I also struggle for air. My new dawn has become dusk, eventide, the cessation of light.

"She will prove it..." he continues, "...at the same time she is busy suing you for malpractice. You spout philosophical nonsense because you're full of it. But you're only trying to wiggle out of a noose you looped around your own neck. Now do what I said. Get the information I want before a concerned citizen acts."

Chapter Twenty-four

Wheels up to wheels down, the flight from LA to Monterey is forty-nine minutes. Add on runway taxi time and some extra minutes of tarmac delay and it's an hour and ten. Once I dig my car out of airport parking, the drive home to Watson Street is another fifteen. All in all, not much longer than a leisurely bike ride along the coast to Lover's Point and back. But it might have been a long-haul flight from LA to Melbourne. I arrive home a bone-weary traveler. I'm not sure where I am, who I am, what has happened.

Weird thoughts plague me. I picture myself like a butterfly with a third wing, as if I have developed some new mode of response to a basic life situation. A kind of original mutation I can't yet consciously evaluate. Why am I thinking these things? I can't say, but I sense the presence of a new strength, a rebirth or revivifying life-force if only I can access it. Besides what Malcolm said about "three" being the perfect number, it is also a traditional symbol of fulfillment, but I don't feel fulfilled. I feel like I've flown off course, lost my bearings in a storm. What happened?

I enter the house and judder to a stop in the living room. Here is the beginning of the storm. A half-eaten sandwich on the coffee table, the television still on, now showing an ad for a vitamin supplement for hair loss. I turn it off, drop my carry-on bag and collapse onto the sofa. I observe the sandwich, the television. So this was how I received the news of Harry's death. An intracranial hemorrhage which left him on the bathroom floor in his robe, a morning hairbrush still in his right hand.

Dimly, I recall packing my bag, booking a flight to LA, racing off to the airport, spending money I do not have on a hotel, then an excruciating dinner with old friends, a hastily made donation to Sylvia, Harry's widow. There was the funeral and afterwards the memorial service, where Sylvia asked me to speak. My stammered phrases, people sobbing. How did I even manage to open my mouth? Maybe that was when I sensed the third wing beginning to grow. Then I flew back to Monterey and now here I am. I know I can't just sit in a storm-tossed living room. I have to move. Stop moving and you die.

I change into my cycling gear, hop onto my bike and coast down the hill into the roar of sea lions. Like the roar in my head. I veer off to the left and pedal along the coastal bike path. Glorious Monterey Bay still stretches out into the Pacific. Blue sky still spans blue water. Gray whales glide by on their migration from the Bering Sea. Perfection through sacrifice but it is no longer harvest time. Winter has become real, the moon still mad. Passing San Carlos Beach, I realize my head is bare. I thought I put my helmet on. Maybe I just looked at it. If I have an accident, I'll crack my brain open and die like Harry. Instead of a hairbrush, I'll clutch a bicycle handle grip. I can't remember if a helmet is required by law. The police could issue a ticket, one I can't afford to pay.

I pause at Cannery Row. A few gulps of water and ten minutes later I roll onto Lovers Point. Two freighters on the horizon heading north, probably to San Francisco or Oakland, but maybe farther on, to Portland or Seattle, maybe even Vancouver or the Aluetians where the whales come from. And who cares? Why do I consider such things or even notice the freighters? Easy answer. The distraction blankets the pain in my heart, the chill in my bones. Dear friend Harry, dear mentor, I promise I won't slip into cornmeal mush and mawkish melodrama but I mourn and miss you. The words I stammered at your memorial service were commands directed at myself. No wonder I could barely pronounce a phrase before choking up. I used your life to describe the value of truth and honesty. Lofty phrases while my imagination envisioned your corpse on the floor, the hairbrush in your hand.

Now here I stand before the boundless Pacific on the brink of my own abyss. I take out my cell phone. I can't resist a final look. I open the last video Harry sent, recorded weeks ago, a ten-second, self-filmed clip. At arm's length, his smiling face appears. Handsome, cheerful, still alive. "Hey," he says. "Here on Sunset and couldn't help thinking about the time you and I..."

I store the clip and reluctantly check my messages, which I haven't looked at in two days. One from the

Garcias, two from another client, four from Beth, and twenty or thirty from Malcolm. I shiver at his inhuman doggedness. Ferocious, stop-at-nothing mania. He will never relent, never let go. So I must yank my soul out of grief and hopelessness, straighten my back and name the game. If he won't let go, I must. As simple as that. I open his most recent email, avoid reading it and quickly type:

Malcolm, this is to inform you that I do not believe I can be of any further use to you. Accordingly, I am officially calling an end to our therapeutic sessions. I wish you all the best. Sincerely, Ryan Mathiesson.

I am not so dauntless that I can resist a moment of hesitation. I look at a passing pelican, at a breaking wave, at nothing in particular. I think of Harry. Finally, I hit Send.

The following afternoon sunlight streams into my consultation office, setting dust motes afloat over the triangle of chairs where I sit with the Garcias. Elbows on armrests, Mr. and Mrs. Garcia lean toward me. They listen with extreme attention because I am speaking to them about the art of listening. As I go on, I experience an expanding sense of gratification. I want to get things back in order, get back to normal life, and this is what I should be doing: caring for my clients. In the end, it is how I can best care for myself. When I pause, Mr. Garcia admits that he is an "expert at nodding."

"Could you elaborate a bit?" I say.

"Elaborate?"

"Yes."

"Is that how they talk in shrink school? Nobody talks like that in real life."

"Then you tell me. How do they talk?"

"They say, 'Can you talk about it some more?'"

"Okay, can you talk about it some more?"

"Sure. My wife, lots of times she talks in circles. Ask her yourself."

I look at Mrs. Garcia who blinks her eyes rapidly, an expression I interpret as reluctant agreement. Mr. Garcia goes on to explain that he learned to use nodding behavior many years ago when he discovered that it satisfied his wife. While she goes on talking, he nods as if paying attention but thinks about other matters: changes he would like to make to his business, this year's MLB batting title and who might win, or a vintage Ford pickup he sometimes sees on the street near his health club. He admits this makes him a "stereotype kind of guy" but only because his wife is a "stereotype kind of gal." What comes first, he asks, the guy and gal or the guy and gal stereotype?

"What comes first is communication," I answer. "Listening without nodding and speaking without putting people to sleep."

They lean farther forward as I describe how to maintain eye contact, be attentive, keep an open mind.

Meanwhile, I continue to feel relief, a sense that in this act of speaking to the Garcias, my life is returning to normal. But then Mr. Garcia says: "Are you all right?"

"What?"

"You look really sad today."

"More than sad," Mrs. Garcia adds. "Like a little boy lost at the carnival. You know, all frightened and lonely scared."

"Now you're listening too well," I say with a laugh, but neither of them join in.

"You should talk about it," Mrs. Garcia says. "Go ahead. We won't interrupt. We'll listen how you said. You know, with good attention and good eye contact."

They stare at me, eyes bulging so far out over their cheek bones I think they have to be joking. But, no, they are so serious I feel compelled to share a word about my trip to LA and Harry's passing.

"The death of a loved one is a terrible thing," Mr. Garcia says. "Even for a shrink."

I curse myself for slipping into the personal. Is this how I return my life to normal? I try to get the session back on track but Mrs. Garcia now has a tear running off her nose. I search through my desk for a tissue. She dabs at her face, I mumble a few final words and then lead them out the door. As we pass Reception, Sheila lowers her gaze. At the lobby entrance, I shake hands first with Mrs. Garcia, then with Mr. Garcia.

"It was good to listen to you," he says, "but it's only

fair that you charge us half price today. I mean, I never heard of patients giving therapy to their shrink."

A moment later, I stand at reception. Eyes still lowered, Sheila lowers her voice as well and tells me I must "proceed immediately" to see President Frederick Kline. That didn't take long, I think. I thank her and start walking. In Kline's office I learn that Ms. Susan Colburne, shark lawyer, has notified the Monterey Counseling Center of intent to file a malpractice suit. Frederick swivels his computer screen around and shows me three photos. Like three wings, I think. Broken wings. One photo of Beth and I on the coastal path. Another of us on the beach holding hands. A third in *The Coastal Quarterly* office naked and making love.

Frederick's face is white, his hands shake on his desk. He explains that the Center cannot tolerate such behavior. As he goes on talking, I catch myself behaving like Mr. Garcia, not listening, just nodding.

I leave Kline's office and walk back out into the lobby. Sheila conveniently has papers to file and must turn her back as I pass. Jenny stands near the entrance to the opposite hallway, observing me worriedly. I should feel scorching ignominy but all I can think is that I do not have the money to hire people to move my belongings out of my office. Somehow I will have to do it myself. My life has just become anything but normal. I am the portrait Mrs. Garcia painted. Lost at the carnival, all frightened and lonely scared.

CHAPTER TWENTY-FIVE

Yesterday I wasn't able to feel shame. Today I can't feel anything but. I carry boxes of books down the hall, through the lobby and out to my car, passing other Counseling Center therapists. They are the same friendly, warm-hearted people who attended the child psychologist's party. Every one of them would normally leap forward to help with my load. But they pass me by without a sideways glance. In the act of shaming myself, I have besmirched their reputations as well. All of them are now therapists who potentially screw their client's spouses.

The only exception is Jenny, who upheaves a stack of files and follows me through the lobby's gauntlet of glaring eyes. Back in the office, we pause in front of my desk and the three armchairs, which are beyond the holding power of my car.

"Ryan, listen," Jenny says. "My nephew is a little rat with an old dropside van and nothing to do. He can bring one of his rat friends and we can load this up and have done with it."

An offer I am in no position to refuse. Yes, please, get me out of here and far away from more shame. She makes a call and an hour later her nephew, whose face really does resemble a rat's visage, appears with a rodent-like friend. Surly eighteen-year-olds reeking of marijuana fumes and unwashed clothes but they obey Jenny's commands and we cart desk, armchairs, rugs and wall hangings up to Watson Street, where my living room gets rearranged into my new consultation office. All I need now are some clients. Only that.

I hand Jenny's nephew the last twenty-dollar bill in my wallet. He grunts at my misery and Jenny walks him out to the street where I'm sure she slips him a few more twenties. At least I still have some wine in the kitchen and can offer her a glass. We sit in the triangle of armchairs and toast to "life's changes."

"On the positive side," Jenny says, "you'll save a fortune on rent."

Any other day and her cheery, upbeat smile would drive me halfway to the ceiling, but I crave light in the tunnel of self-disgust. I also sense a presence in the third armchair. The empty armchair. Who is it now—Harry, Beth, Malcolm? Maybe the self I used to be. Jenny and I share a second glass of wine, chat about this and that, and in the middle of chatting I begin to realize we are on our way to the bedroom. She has the same presentiment, I'm sure. I should be terrified of the risk, terrified of adding one more gram of chaos to my life, but what life worth living is without risk? An attractive woman is within arm's reach. I can't just sit on my hands.

Another sip of wine, and I inch forward on the cushion, reach over and set my hand on her knee. She picks up my hand and caresses it warmly. A moment passes before I realize her caress is loving and tender but in no way sexual. Her eyes open in puzzled surprise as she murmurs *oh*, and releases my hand.

"I thought... I mean, it's no secret," she says. "Everyone knows..."

Turns out she's gay. No secret, everyone knows. Oh. She mumbles a pat phrase about being flattered and we chat some more and then she rises to leave. I walk her to the door, where I hug her—very clumsily—and she exits stage left.

Back in my armchair, I take a large gulp of wine and proceed to castigate myself. The worst part is I didn't listen to my own warning about more chaos. I was too smart for that, too much the daredevil risk-taker.

I wanted to distance myself from more shame and now I picture Jenny telling the story at the Counseling Center, my former colleagues, even Frederick Kline, bent double in raging laughter. Thank all the sea lions, I don't have to return there. But, no, she's not the type to share the scene and nothing horrendous occurred. Just more blindness on my part. I didn't see what everyone else saw. Of course, now I see the obvious everywhere, in all her mannerisms, actions, attitudes.

So what to do? When in doubt, check your cell phone. One message from Beth. Not a word from Malcolm since I terminated our sessions. Terminated them by email, the coward's way out. Now he sends messages via the shark. Has he told Beth about me snooping and poking into her desk? More likely he'll hold that hard kernel of info like a hammer over my head, ready to drop when he sees fit. I can remove the threat by telling Beth myself, but that's not on my agenda for today. Maybe not tomorrow either.

So now that I have checked my cell, what next? When in doubt, go for a bike ride. I pedal across Monterey, telling myself direction doesn't matter. Just pedal and ride anywhere, but an hour later I find I have traveled a direct route to the edge of Del Monte Forest. I put on the brakes and glide to a stop—panting, dripping sweat— in a cypress grove. Hidden among the trees, I observe a chain link fence and Pacific House in the distance beyond. No movement I can discern either within or without the house.

I wipe sweat out of my eyes, but can't mute the ocean's thunder in my ears. I once wondered why Beth let Malcolm stay, why she didn't have security throw him out on his nose. Instead, she helped him into therapy, tried to wash her hands of him, get away physically and psychically, always, no doubt, with a hammer over her head as well. Has she filed for divorce yet? No, because "the man is dying," but really she's terrified of the hammer. Just like me.

I look down at my hands still squeezing the rubber grips. Time to admit Malcolm has been gaslighting me as well. My poor soul, where has it gone? I take out my phone and call Beth, my twin soul, or so we've said. The signal is bad in the woods but the crackles and faint slapbacks serve my purpose. Between fade outs, I tell her I need some time alone after Harry's death. She hesitates, then says, "Remember I'm here, just a call away..." Now I'm not sure if it is her voice or the signal which is weak. "And just a little reminder," she adds encouragingly, "we have the final interview coming up."

"No problem," I say. Huge problem. Last thing I want to do. I can't imagine sitting on the hot seat—near her desk—beneath the omniscient fisheye gaze of the security camera—wielding her clever questions. No longer the shining Esalen therapist-hero, just another disgraced wannabe. Once she knows the truth, will she still want to interview me? Probably. I'm committed and it's been announced. At stake is the reputation of *The Coast Quarterly* and whatever's left of my own rep as well.

I stare at Pacific House for another minute. Impossible to see anything, so I turn and start pushing the bike through the woods. I pass a hiker, a birdwatcher, a man sitting near the base of a cypress munching on pistachios. People are California affable. They smile, say hello, tell me it's a great day, a great place to be. A jack rabbit bounds through the undergrowth, hops over a fallen trunk, darts into a thicket and disappears. I come to a small clearing where a family is enjoying a picnic. They wave across the way. I wave back, the cordial cyclist. There are two boys. The older boy is busy digging a hole near his parents. The youngest boy, about four or five, stands apart, staring up at the sky. What is he looking at? Not a cloud, not a bird, not an airplane in sight. Then I realize he is staring in supreme wonder at a single autumn leaf dangling from the upper branches of a tree.

I mount my bike and pedal through the rest of the forest. I need to see better, farther, deeper.

CHAPTER TWENTY-SIX

Bless Mr. and Mrs. Garcia who I wanted to drop as clients. Bless their troubled marriage. Neither husband nor wife have the slightest compunction over continuing our sessions in my living room. "Same comfy chairs," Mr. Garcia says, "and if you ask me, that other joint was too highfalutin." "I like these cushions," Mrs. Garcia adds, "except for too many butt dimples."

At the end of our session I am tempted to tell them that my other clients have fled the coop, but instead I announce unexpected open appointments in my schedule. Three hours later—bless Mr. and Mrs. Garcia—I begin to receive calls from their friends. The friends seem to have something in common. Mr. and Mrs. Martínez. Mr. and Mrs. López. Mr. and Mrs. Sánchez. Bless them all. They won't save my ship from sinking but they'll keep it bouncing above water a while longer.

That afternoon I walk down to the Wharf and pause within sight of the Counseling Center. "Jenny was right," I tell myself. "No more rent." I go into Abalonetti's, sit harbor side by a large window and drink a beer. A text message arrives from Beth but I'm not ready to face her, even on a screen. I watch seals and sea lions float between the moored yachts. What was the Kerouac line Beth quoted that day? I can't remember. Before long, she sends a second message. I turn off my phone. I still have to trudge back up to the house so I probably shouldn't order another beer but I do. When I leave, maybe I'll keel over on the hill and roll all the way back down straight into the drink with the seals.

Twenty minutes later, I finish the beer, which wasn't as tasty as I thought it might be, and force myself out the door. Yawning, I start marching up the hill. I reach Watson Street and make for home. In the next moment I spot a figure on the lawn chair on my front porch. It's Beth, pen in hand, manuscript on her lap, brow creased. At the sound of my feet dragging on the sidewalk, she looks up, removes her reading glasses. The curtains behind her are open, offering a clear view into the living room. She couldn't have missed the three armchairs. How do I begin an explanation? I mount the porch stairs and stop in front of her, now face to face but still not ready. She makes no movement toward me. I don't know what to say or do. I hesitate, then step forward and press my lips onto hers.

"Not a very enthusiastic kiss," I say.

"Malcolm called a dozen times," she replies dryly. "When I refused to answer my phone, he sent an enormous email. He told me you went through my desk. He said I could verify it on security footage."

My body shakes and the world blurs. Now I really might keel over and roll back down into the Bay. But, overwhelmed by guilt and remorse, I perceive an oddity.

She's angry, not furious. Or her fury is contained. She glances around the porch, takes a breath, then admits she lied to me as well. She tells me she has always lied about money, as far back as boarding school when she dressed in medium-priced sweatshirts and jeans and tried to look like everyone else, but the other girls smelled the bankroll in her background and used to hit her up for five dollars here, ten dollars there. They disliked her if she didn't loan the money, hated her if she asked for it back. Excuses didn't protect her but lies did. When she entered Yale, an aunt advised her to let the Dijkstra Foundation take over the management of her affairs and she has maintained the arrangement ever since.

"I'm so used to lying about my money," she says. "I believe the lie myself."

We stand before each other on the open porch, wounds exposed. Whoever we thought we were, we are not. Twin liars. And hers isn't just a boarding-school lie. It's a confidence she could have shared. But she chose not to, probably had me stuffed into the same pigeonhole with Malcolm: another deceitful male.

"It has to stop here," she says. "Right now, this minute. Cease contact. No more therapy sessions, no calls, no emails, no messages. He'll find the key to open the lock. He always does. It's how he breaks people down. By debasing them. It makes it easier for him to force them to do something again. And again."

Her anger doesn't cover her pain and it pains me to become its witness. I force myself not to look away. I knew I had to start over after Harry's death, but never imagined this would be the starting point. My lover and I unearthing our flaws. Now we either abandon the garden or overturn tainted soil and plant anew.

"If you haven't told him about the Dijkstra Foundation," Beth continues, "he's no better off than he was a week ago. On the contrary, he's worse off every day. But he won't back down, we can count on that."

"I'll handle him," I say.

"Nobody can handle him. Don't even think about it. Besides, you're in no shape to handle anything. You look tired. Death will handle him. Leave it at that. I have to go."

I thank her for coming over. She could have decided not to, could have kept her own lie hidden and left me hung out to dry. I kiss her and this time she kisses back.

"That's better," I say.

She graces me with a faint smile and leaves. But she only makes it halfway down the steps before turning back around. "Ryan, please remember what I said. Don't go anywhere near him."

I watch her leave, then I enter the house and head for one of the armchairs. I am raw and wasted. I know she feels the same but there's nothing I can do about that now. It's time to stop, I tell myself. I need to take a long, luxurious nap. I sit down, close my eyes and drift peacefully for several minutes, but then I begin to fidget. I stand up. Beth might think it all ends by ceasing contact with Malcolm but she said it herself: he won't back down. Aside from that, there's the little matter of some lawsuits. So nothing has changed. And nothing will until I stop him.

More turbulent thoughts send me into a whirl and then out to the car. I drive to Walmart and park near the entrance. Inside, I find a section dedicated to telescopes and binoculars. The clerk reminds me of Jenny's 18-year-old nephew, though more than a rat he resembles an arrogant duck. He points out a few telescopes and begins to talk about angular resolution and concave mirrors, about magnification and light gathering ability. He asks, "Would you describe yourself as an amateur astronomer or an outdoor enthusiast?"

"I'm not sure..." He's making me more tired than I already am.

"Then let's put it this way. Do you want to see planets or stars?"

So the lecture about magnification was to impress me and now we have sarcasm. He thinks I'm some kind of mindless telescope rookie.

"I'd like to see well enough," I reply, "to distinguish desire from destiny."

He doesn't even bat a duck eyelash. Just gives me a knowing smirk as he reaches for one of the cheap, handheld models. I pay up and leave, grateful that my credit card still works. Back at the house, I again head for an armchair. This time with fewer thoughts but then I decide what I really need is the sofa. Within minutes, I am sound asleep. When I awake an hour later, I discover that I am holding the telescope in my right hand. I am sluggish and under the effects of an especially vivid dream in which an eagle and a large white dove changed into each other.

I roll upward into a sitting position. I studied dream analysis under Harry Higby's guidance but I was never very interested, so never very adept. The stories my clients recounted were dreamy enough. I didn't need to dip into their nocturnal lives. But this dream lingers. I still see the eagle and dove as they become one another. It might be a kind of Yin-Yang interplay. A willful eagle and a loving dove, but the same purpose. Or who knows? Maybe the telescope made me think of the expression "eagle-eyed" and reminded me of Malcolm's cane. I raise the telescope and examine it more closely.

Chapter Twenty-seven

I should have paid closer attention to the arrogant duck's lecture on magnification. Pacific House looms like a galleon on a dark sea and my cheap telescope leaves me out of range. The planets and stars, desire and destiny are beyond reach. Hazy lights glow in the distant night, that's all. One of the sitting rooms, I think, or maybe the sunroom with the yellow chaise lounge.

Time passes. The forest creeks behind me. I can't resist turning to look. Will I behold the ghost deer? No, not even a swaying branch. But the shadowed trees remind me that King Arthur and his knights used to hunt for a white stag in the woods. The knight who captured the creature, a symbol of elusive purity, could bestow a kiss on the fairest lady at court. The shadows put weird thoughts into my head, a chill into my bones. Do I seek a fair lady or am I only acting crazy? I unscrew the lid to my thermos, take two sips of black coffee, bite into a ham sandwich. The hot liquid restores my resolve. I tell myself the worst that can happen is I'll catch a cold. No, the worst would be Beth finding out. Then I lose it all. Fool me once, shame on you. The fair lady won't forgive twice.

The lights go off around midnight. Dim security lights flick on near the front and rear entrances. I wait another fifteen minutes and then leave. I haven't seen a thing. Am I wasting my time? Almost certainly, but I return the following night. I creep through the woods and then crouch beneath two Monterey cypresses. The position is similar to last night's but closer to the chain link fence.

Pacific House appears no different. Majestic, remote, unknown. What is it that I don't see? I drink coffee and munch on a sandwich. At least I haven't been crazy enough to go back to Walmart and buy a more expensive telescope. No moon tonight, or the fog has engulfed it the same as the stars. The ocean is out of sight, obscured by rising land, yet still rumbling darkly. I think I see movement in the house but it is a pinpoint of light shimmering in the darkness, nothing more. Later, there is another movement, more distinct. I raise the telescope and press my eye firmly into the narrow-view eyepiece. Hard to say what it might have been; maybe the wheelchair rolling down a corridor past a window. One thing for sure: a tripod would have been useful. The cold tube jiggles in my hand. I swear in a whisper. The movement does not repeat.

My thoughts wander to Beth. Staring at Pacific House, I fear the third and final interview will be truly final. I should be preparing for it now. Instead, I sit in a forest on a cold night. What will she ask me? What answers can I give when I am empty even of echoes?

Every now and then I sweep the telescope across the property, to the right and left and back again. No sign of security. Does the guard make rounds during the night or just sit warm and cozy in his guard booth? How many monitors does he have in front of him, all of them showing shadow and darkness? Maybe he's drinking coffee and munching on a sandwich like me. The lights go out around midnight.

The third and fourth nights are no different. The fifth night finds me once again hidden in the shadows beneath the two cypresses. A breeze off the ocean makes branches quiver. Overhead, the sliver of an Aries moon appears, not very bright, the last slim bow of a waxing crescent. I spot an airplane sailing past, high in the night sky. The sight ignites a chain of futile thinking about the third interview. In the first two, I struggled to sound like the person I had once been. Now I must be the person I'll become.

Looking back at Pacific House, I discover a new light switched on near the middle of the structure. When did that happen? I missed it when I was gazing at the plane. I raise the telescope and observe a blur of movement. What room is that? I can't remember and can't visualize walking through the house. Too many rooms, too many corridors. The movement continues. I seem to distinguish two forms, then everything blurs again. I'm not sure what causes the blur, distance or my eye pressed too hard into the eyepiece, but the result is the same: obscurity.

I let frustration eat at me for five minutes and then I

step out from beneath the trees. I creep toward the fence. I tell myself that security cameras can't possibly cover every inch of the property and even if they do, nobody will watch the footage. Like *The Coastal Quarterly* office, security personnel will only review footage if there has been some kind of incident, a theft or break in. Besides, at this hour the guard is probably half asleep or watching a film on his laptop.

I push the telescope through the galvanized mesh and clamber over the fence, scraping my arm on the way down. I pause to catch my breath and steel my nerve, listening to the soft thunderous roar of the ocean. Then I pick up the telescope and set off across the fog-dampened ground. Twice, I stop to check the shadows near the house. I wonder if the security guard has a dog, a Doberman that can smell and hear anything. I angle toward the newly lighted room, cautioning myself not to get too close. Along with security cameras there are probably motion detectors. I thought I observed two figures moving inside the house. Now I'm not sure. I sneak closer. Yes, there are two figures. One is a man, the other a woman. My god, is it Beth?

I stop in my tracks. There must be some explanation. Of course, it's her house. She can come and go whenever she wants. Maybe Malcolm has finally died and she has taken back her rightful residence. It's still hard to tell from the distance but she seems to hold a drink in one hand, a stick in the other. It's the billiard room, I realize.

I pass it every time I go through the house. I should have known. Two steps closer and I come to my senses. I remember I hold the telescope in my hand. I raise it to my right eye. The woman is blond. She is attired in a strapless cocktail dress, dark blue with lace and a pearl necklace. She appears wealthy, sexy, effete. She bears a resemblance from a distance, that's all. She is not Beth.

But there is no mistaking the man as he saunters around the pool table eyeing the position of the balls. He stands tall and upright just as he did the day of our first session on the cliff edge, now gripping a pool cue instead of an eagle-beaked cane. He throws a winning smile at the woman. I remain in a penumbra of shadow just beyond the light which floods out from the room onto the nearby ground. I can't risk getting any closer. Yet all I need to see is here. I have gone from staring at a blur to observing every tiny object in detail. Malcolm leans forward onto the table. He makes a circle with his thumb and index finger and inserts the cue through the circle to rest on top of his middle finger, just behind the knuckle. His movements are precise and assured. He spreads out the tips of his ring and middle fingers and creates a support. He shoots, balls scatter and he stands upright, smiling. The woman sets aside her drink and pool cue and claps elegantly, acknowledging his triumph with a fashionable shrug of her bare shoulders. I run the telescope over Malcolm's clothes. He sports a beige dinner jacket and maroon silk ascot. Smoothly and authoritatively, he approaches the woman. They kiss lightly. They stare into each other's eyes. I can't see the woman's face but Malcolm's expression is confident, loving, gentle. Charming beyond belief. He shows the woman exactly what she wants to see. They kiss again more passionately.

I become aware of the roar of the ocean. I stumble backward. I have to get away. I recall the terror in Yetta's eyes. I feel the same. I turn and retreat across the damp ground, careful not to hurry, careful not to step on anything that might cause me to trip or make a sound. I no longer imagine the guard snoozing in front of his monitors. Now I imagine him sprinting across the field toward me, drawing his gun, a Doberman racing along at his side.

I push the telescope through the fence. I don't know if I have the strength to pull my weight up over the top bar. My arms tremble. I throw my right leg over the bar and look back across the yard. Nothing but darkness. The house lights are off. The game of pool has ended.

I drop to the ground and scramble for the two cypress trees. Once again hidden in the shadows, I crouch like a stone statue. I try to calm my breathing. There is no movement in the darkness beyond the fence, no security guard or Doberman. Still, I continue peering into the night, thinking that I sensed it, knew it, felt it in my gut. I don't have to ask Beth if she ever accompanied Malcolm to his oncological appointments. If she did, he told her to wait in the cafeteria, in the car, in some nearby place while he prepared a mask of grief and worry to meet her again. She has been wrong from the start. This isn't just another mask. It isn't just a man who feigns illness in a wheelchair. It is malevolence. It is evil.

I pick up my thermos, the telescope, the remains of my sandwich. Grasping everything, I lurch forward into the woods.

CHAPTER TWENTY-EIGHT

Yetta opens the front door to Pacific House and stands aside. She is dressed in a light blue uniform. A pastel-colored alligator clip holds her hair at the side. I greet her by name, ask how she is.

Gaze lowered, she murmurs, "Yes, thank you, fine..."

"You will be," I reply and for an instant she raises her eyes.

She leads me down the central corridor. We pass the sunroom, the library, the marble statuary, and come to the billiard room, where I pause. Except for a bit of lint shining on the pool table's green felt, there is nothing unusual about the room, but I observe it a moment longer. Yetta regards me quizzically and then I follow her through the west wing and into the kitchen. The sliding glass door is already open. I start across the yard, heading toward the outcropping where Malcolm sits in his wheelchair. I take long slow steps. No gardener today but I feel that I am not alone, that some community, visible or not, sustains my efforts. The sea is glassy near the horizon, choppy along the shore running northward. Malcolm sits hunched forward in the wheelchair, dark eyes fixed on my approach. He is part of some community too, I think. Or was.

In my entire life I have only thrown two punches. Both when I was a teenager. One was an uppercut which missed a chin by a foot and the other was a roundhouse haymaker that clubbed an adolescent enemy to the sidewalk. I've imagined using the same wild punch to send Malcolm flying out of his wheelchair. I've pictured him sprawled across the ground or stretched spread-eagle over the flat granite boulder. I've seen my hands at his throat, wringing his neck as he gasps for breath.

But I must resist even the vaguest temptation of such fantasies. My courage must be supreme or I'll be annihilated. I must do nothing. I must take no pleasure, achieve not the slightest satisfaction. I can't raise my voice or gesture abruptly. No matter how I rage inside, I will speak in a gentle tone, hide behind my own mask, a mild-mannered accountant delivering a humdrum monthly financial report. Profits are slightly up, investments stable, rates of return likely to be positive. I have no other choice. To get to who I want to be, I must go through him.

I arrive at the granite boulder and take my seat. Malcolm is dressed in his Bottega Veneta robe. Bent forward under the guise of false illness, he emits suppressed menace and mounting threat. I sense that he is also containing himself, that he is purely focused on destroying me.

"I have sent you messages," he begins slowly, "and you have not answered me. Unless you think your last message was an answer. It wasn't. I told you what would transpire if you did not provide the Pacific House

Agreement. I made the consequences very clear. Did you think I would allow you to escape without paying the price I named?"

Once again, waves pound the rocks at the base of the cliff. I act as if the noise has prevented me from hearing his words. I appear somewhat impatient, an accountant with another meeting on his busy schedule, a meeting far more important than this one. I must get some trivial items out of the way before I leave, that's all.

"Our sessions have ended," I say, "as I made clear to you. But I've come to give you a final piece of advice."

"I do not want or need your advice. I want and need the Pacific House Agreement. Produce it or suffer the consequences. I tire of repeating this. The sessions will end when I say. Not before. There are still actions you are required to take. The third interview in my wife's little magazine. No matter what she asks, you will give certain answers. It will be amusing. I will tell you what you must say."

I wave my hand as if we are talking about some event in the remote past. "The interview's already finished. Already taped and edited and at the printers. In a few days the new issue will be in bookstores. Now listen for a second because I'm in a hurry and don't have time to waste."

Any reaction would indicate loss of control, so he gives no reaction. He doesn't even blink one of his hooded eyes. What if I jumped forward and smashed my fist into his face—would he react then? No, I must quell my violence or I will be the one who ends up smashed. I remind myself that he is the path to me.

"After today," I go on, "there will no longer be any contact, not even the possibility of it. No phone calls, no emails, none of your text messages. You need to begin thinking of your future."

His hand squeezes the joystick. "What are you going on about now?"

"I repeat: no contact. You have a week to leave Pacific House premises. It's not much time but I'm sure you'll be able to arrange everything. If not, Dijkstra Foundation Security will arrange it for you in a manner you won't like. If Pacific House has one hair out of place, one missing fork or absent napkin, you'll be held responsible."

He smiles weakly through the veil of bogus disease, but his voice toughens. "My wife is still my wife and she—"

"No, she isn't. All that is finished. It's at the printers as well, officially put to bed. So you need to wake up and listen to what I'm saying. Beth is already long gone, beyond your reach, beyond your control. From now on, as you'll soon learn, you're on your own."

He still gives no sign that he is even slightly affected by my words, but my long lost intuition resurfaces and tells me otherwise. I experience clarity. I've managed to hold myself in check. I can't say I've transcended conflict or encountered the oneness of existence, but I've approached a state of inner assurance.

"Whatever you've done, or think you've done," he replies, "you are the one who will soon learn something. You will learn you have made the mistake of your pathetic life."

His long phrases are now free of his pretense. He no longer feigns coughing or shortness of breath. Nor does he wince from some false stab of pain. I stand up, waving my hand again. "I have to go, Malcolm. Take good care. I'm sorry I couldn't have done more for you."

I should leave it at that and walk off to my imagined meeting of accountants. But I can't. No matter my clarity, no matter my inner assurance, I can't ignore the rage in my gut. I step forward and grasp the lapels of his elegant robe. Even in my fingertips, I sense his shock at someone touching his person. He is caught between resisting and keeping up his show.

"Here, let me help you," I say politely.

Before he can do or even say anything, I yank him upward out of the wheelchair. He is dead weight, paralyzed by the audacity of my act, by the drill of his own act. Grunting, I swing him around in a semi-circular motion—*another dance*, I think—and ease him down onto a sitting position atop the flat granite boulder.

"If we really are being filmed," I say, "this'll make great footage."

I let loose one slap across his face, not a punch, just a stinging rebuke. His dark eyes fly open, turn white. I move to the wheelchair and take hold of the joystick.

The chair spins to the left, jerks forward. I give it a final hard push over the cliff edge. Amid the sound of crashing waves, there comes the sound of crashing metal. I cast a glance at Malcolm. The mask is gone. I start walking across the field toward Pacific House, his murderous, impotent eyes on my back.

Chapter Twenty-nine

*O*ur special marriage-themed issue of The Coast *Quarterly now presents the third and final installment of our ongoing interview with marriage therapist Ryan Mathiesson. Parts One and Two—The Basics and The Metaphysics, respectively—now lead us into Part Three: The Marriage Dance. Once again, Founding Editor Elizabeth Dijkstra sits down with Mathiesson in our Carmel office and together they attempt to tie the knot on this interesting exchange of ideas. The Coast Quarterly also takes this opportunity to announce that Dijkstra will soon begin a well deserved and long-anticipated sabbatical. In her temporary absence, Senior Fiction Editor MaryAnn Baros will assume all responsibilities for running The Coast Quarterly while loyal intern Bernard Kopka becomes our new Assistant Editor. As always, the podcast of the following interview is freely available to subscribers on our webpage.*

ED: In its own humble way, *The Coast Quarterly* believes that literature is mankind's vast and enduring effort to reach for knowledge transferable from generation to generation. Bearing that in mind, I'd now like to delve more deeply into the literature of love. Let's look at what Shelley, Proust, Rilke, Homer and others had to say about the marriage dance and then get your thoughts on their thoughts.

RM: Long before Hollywood became our primary source of education on love and romance, we had literature. A characteristic trait in human nature is the ability to "bind time." It's the ability to transfer to other men and women as yet unborn the harvest of conscious experiences and deliberate endeavors. Nothing does it more preciously than literature.

ED: Homer, the father of western literature, gave us one of the great marital relationships in the history of letters, the myth of Penelope and Odysseus.

RM: The ever-patient motionless soul cries out to the ever-restless wandering spirit.

ED: And how do soul and spirit finally unite? In marriage or homecoming?

RM: There is no difference.

ED: Shelley famously wrote "soul meets soul on lovers' lips..."

RM: A phrase apparently brimming with passion, but we often forget that in the very next line he tells us that this occurs when "High hearts are calm, and brightest eyes are dull..."

ED: Nonetheless, it seems you have just affirmed that soul and spirit do indeed unite, indicating that our perfect lover, our twin flame exists.

RM: As I said before, our quest for the twin flame is a universal desire etched onto our souls. Inherently, instinctively, we seek pure love and spiritual union in a polar opposite.

ED: And what are our chances of discovering this polar opposite, of finding our twin flame?

RM: Slim and getting slimmer. You have only to take a good look at the state of modern courtship to realize we can barely keep a tiny spark alive, never mind a bright burning flame.

ED: I repeat yet again: you tend to sound pessimistic. And I ask again: could it be because of what you see daily in your consultation office?

RM: (reluctantly) Yes, it could.

ED: Then let's diverge for a moment. Tell us what you see.

RM: First, I have to point out that happy couples don't pay me money to make them happier. The people who enter my office have serious problems. Often, they can barely speak to one another any longer. They are so blinded by suffering they can't bear to look the other's way. At best, they pretend to look. What I observe outside of my office—couples in bars, restaurants, at dinner parties, the gas station, the supermarket—reveals the potentiality for the same suffering. Modern life and our own wicked ways have set all of us on the brink of divorce. Even couples who have been together for many years—at one time or other, they have been at the point of dissolution, even if one partner in the couple is unaware of it. Perhaps this state of near rupture has become necessary. Perhaps we must lose faith, betray and separate so that we may heal and come together again.

ED: So a relationship defeated by betrayal can be resurrected?

RM: (hesitates) Yes, and given a new life purpose. Death and rebirth. Beyond any doubt, it is possible if the couple make the effort and saturate their beings with love. That said, my practice has taught me another thing for certain: the notion that we are bound together for life is no longer in anyone's skull, no matter what vows they have made. More than ever before, we know there is no permanence. The state of wedlock has been unlocked.

ED: This recalls the expression to "tie the knot." Proust said, "The bonds that unite another person to our self exist only in the mind." Earlier you spoke of the ability to "bind time."

RM: An ability that transcends instinct and biology. It is based on choice, will and self-sacrifice for the sake of future human beings. It rests upon a deep feeling of the value of community and eventually destroys the roots of loneliness. It makes a life truly "human." Men and women join in the vast process of a living civilization to fulfill the basic implications of the human stage of cosmic evolution.

ED: Now you echo your previous comments on the alchemy of marriage, the potential of relationships to transmute chaos into synergy.

RM: We do so not merely for ourselves but for our children, our friends, relatives, neighbors, strangers, the entire world. A good relationship radiates grace onto all who come near it.

ED: You're beginning to sound more and more optimistic.

RM: We're brought together to dance and that implies optimism. It also implies not stepping on each other's toes and learning the right steps.

ED: What steps?

RM: First, give your dance partner space. Then support. Don't judge the way he or she dances. Rhythm is the thing and you are in it. You are always in the dance. No one is a wallflower. The only difference is that for some the music has already begun; for others, it might start at any moment.

ED: Okay, let's say the dance is under way. What's the next step?

RM: Life begins a second time in the dance, in union. If it manages to begin a second time. Many lives do not. They leave the world as the separate and lonely self in which they entered.

ED: Rilke said, "It is part of the nature of every definitive love that sooner or later it can only reach the beloved in infinity.

RM: Rilke's thoughts on solitude which we spoke of earlier, would make a wonderful vow in a wedding ceremony, even better than "til death do us part." *I hereby vow to protect my lover's solitude.*

ED: So what's the trick? How do we meet our perfect lover? How will you Ryan Mathiesson, expert marriage therapist—how will you recognize your perfect lover?

RM: I can't know until it happens—if it happens—but perhaps I'll recognize her by the questions she asks.

ED: (hesitates) You said before that we must make ourselves ready. Let's assume we've done that. Let's assume we're ready to dance. Then what? Do we suddenly bump into our dance partner on the street?

RM: Lovers don't meet by chance. They meet by magic, a magic so powerful it overwhelms and feels like it has existed forever. As if the lovers have been in each other all along. This isn't sugarcoated, sticky-sweet romantic talk. Anyone who has ever fallen in love knows it as fact. The magic is there and it has been there waiting all along.

ED: It sounds like we just entered the ballroom of destiny. Of fated encounter. What comes next—a waltz? A tango?

RM: Rock 'n' roll. We no longer have the patience to await destiny like some alchemy sent from the stars. We open our hearts and souls, fling out our arms, kick up our heels and boogie till we drop.

ED: What happened to solitude?

RM: That's the marriage. That's the dance: two solitudes in a wild loving twirl.

Chapter Thirty

I don't like visiting Pacific House, even if it's only once a week to check on things. I barely stay an hour but the place makes me feel an ache I resist calling loneliness. That's what I felt when Harry died. This is different. Still, it's hard to find another emotion in this royal residence of rooms without end. I wander the corridors, murmuring Beth's name. Capacious silence echoes back. I have become who I am: a motionless soul crying out to a wandering spirit. She will return, I think. I must make myself ready.

Down at the point, I linger near the flat granite boulder, contemplating waves through gaps in the fog. Gray whales now pass by every few days on their voyage of sacrifice from the Bering Sea, still a thousand miles from their winter breeding grounds in Baja. I can usually distinguish their behemoth shapes among the monstrous waves but today the fog plays tricks on my eyes.

Beth was certain Malcolm would never stop until he had hunted her down, until he had taken full possession of Pacific House and made it his own. I feared he would exact vengeance, that he would be unable to resist the pleasure of destroying us. My only hope was that as the months went by his obsession might wane. Both Beth and I were wrong. It took less than a week. Malcolm was a half dozen steps ahead of us. I even witnessed his groundwork, though I didn't know it at the time. His new lover, his new victim, was his late night pool partner, the elegant blond woman. She is Amahle Deckster-Anjou, a widow and the scion of a South African jewelry empire. She resides in Orchard Manor, a fabulous estate near Morro Bay, just north of San Luis Obispo, a two-hour drive to the south. Malcolm sent me one text message from his new residence. A single sentence. "Orchard Manor is twice the size and value of Pacific House."

His declaration of victory. It still turns my stomach. I refuse to believe he can so easily run off without even a wrinkle to a new mask. Simply the ways of the world? I refuse to believe that as well, even at the risk of naïveté. Meanwhile, I'm grateful for small blessings. Contrary to my fears, Malcolm muzzled his shark lawyer, so no charges were ever filed. Feasting at a new banquet, he no longer cares about crumbs left behind. No doubt, he also wants to avoid any scandals that might jeopardize future meals.

Frederick Kline acted much the same. Glad to be rid of me, he left it at that. No public condemnation, no professional censure. Nothing that might bring a shadow of ill repute onto the Monterey Counseling Center. So my name was cleared not by proof of innocence, but by lack of accusation.

Then my interview in *The Coast Quarterly* came out. Soon after, I received a call from *The Californian*, the digital and print publication which covers the Salinas Valley. They have contracted me to write a monthly column for their Sunday supplement pertaining to any aspect of marriage I may wish. They asked me to remember that *The Californian* does not enjoy the same highbrow readership as *The Coast Quarterly*. In announcing the forthcoming column, they have described me as "controversial." Beth says "controversial" in modern parlance means "interesting." Another call came from Esalen, of all places, suggesting I pick up where I left off years ago. A second workshop, also whatever I may wish, highbrow or not.

So I have gone from no options on the table to puzzling over the kind of workshop I might conduct. I keep imagining three mounds of knowledge on my head. *The Basics, The Metaphysics,* and *The Marriage Dance.* I can't conceive of speaking of much else, but I fear Esalen wants me to act like some kind of relationship philosopher. Poking through Beth's books on my last visit, I read that a true philosopher is a man able to understand, not merely know, the processes of life as he comes to experience them directly. He is the man of wisdom, different from the man of science. It made me think of my long-ago self, how ready and willing I was to bequeath my vast pool of knowledge onto others. These days I'm not so ready. Maybe that indicates an ounce of wisdom.

I check my watch. Eleven AM. Beth is just preparing

her dinner. I have a session with the Garcias and then I will observe her sipping a cup of tea before she starts getting ready for bed. I take a last look at the fog-driven sea. The other night I read that low frequency whale songs can travel 10,000 miles, double the distance to my lover. Of course, you have to be able to hear the frequency.

Up at the house, I exchange a word with Yetta. The absent lines on her forehead and the ever-so-slight upturning of her lips express the changed mood of Pacific House. In a matter of weeks, she has gone from being terrified to being bored. As usual, she asks if I know when Beth will return.

"Soon," I answer. "Very soon."

I go to Beth's study on the opposite side of the house. It's a small room with an antique desk, dark oak bookshelves and a fireplace, like a miniature version of *The Coast Quarterly* office. More old world flair. A large horizontal window shows a distant patch of fog hovering above a patch of ocean. The painting "Solicitude" hangs on the far wall. It's not as big as I imagined when Beth first described it, about a foot square, but the child giving water to birds now reminds me of the ghost deer. The same elusive purity. I return two books to the shelves and borrow two more. Then I lift "Solicitude" off it's hook on the wall and leave Pacific House for good.

Back in Monterey, I tidy up my living room. Looking over the three armchairs, I recall my three mounds of knowledge. The Garcias arrive and we talk about the importance of conflict resolution, parenting skills and a shared social life. The session goes well. Afterwards I walk them out to their car. We shake hands and say goodbye but Mr. Garcia grimaces as he looks back at the house.

"Look at them boards peeling and flaking," he says. "Your shack needs a coat of paint."

Straight-faced, I reply: "I'd have to up my prices for that."

"At it again," Mrs. Garcia scolds her husband. "Giving ideas no one wants and that we have to pay for."

They climb into their car still snapping at each other. I watch them drive off down Watson Street. They will be together forever, I think. They are my parents.

Back in the house, I pour a glass of water and go to my computer. At exactly 1:30 PM California time, Beth's face appears on the screen. Steam rises off a tea mug on a table in front of her. Through the steam, she blows me a kiss.

"Hey," she says.

"Hey, yourself," I reply. "How are things?"

"Great...truly great... but there's a slight change in plans."

My heart sinks. "You're not coming. Please don't tell me that."

"They've asked me to help organize a New Year's Day poetry reading to coincide with the marathon reading at

The Poetry Project in New York. It'll be in both French and English."

"You can respectfully decline."

"No, I can't. Really I can't. Not after all they've done. But maybe you could come here instead. We switch roles, that's all. I promise you'll love it, at least love being loved by me. Do you have a passport?"

Every Skype call pulls her farther away. Initially, she was to teach one class in comparative literature and translation. A camouflage of academia to conceal her escape from Malcolm's wrath. Then the Sorbonne offered her a graduate seminar in the artistic management of a literary magazine. They are impressed with her, it seems, or maybe they just hope to land an impressive donation from the Dijkstra Foundation. In either case, they are making things easy for her transition into French life. They have found her a tiny office on the edge of the Latin Quarter, a short walk from her classes, and arranged for her membership in an equestrian club in Neuilly-sur-Marne. As if icing on the European cake, she is also collaborating with the literary magazine, *Lever du soleil,* to bring out a special French poetry issue of *The Coast Quarterly.* She hopes to arrange an interview with Valérie Rouzeau, a recipient of the *Prix Guilluame-Apollinaire.* So her sabbatical has translated into long distance online work. She is in touch with MaryAnn and Bernie every day of the week. Here on the solitary edge of the windblown Pacific, open spaces in all directions, she couldn't breathe. Now, in the heart of a crowded and polluted city, she breathes freely.

She tells me there is a shop down the street from her apartment that rents bicycles to tourists. "We can pedal into the new year together."

"It sounds wonderful," I say. "But we need to meet on some middle ground first."

"You mean an island in the Atlantic? Imagine pedaling together through the Bois. It's like an island. It'll be fun, romantic, healthy, *merveilleux!*"

Her enthusiasm is genuine and her smile a delight, but she has kept her sanity through the whole ordeal by keeping her nose in books. She's not yet ready to dance. Nor am I. We need what I often tell my clients: more processing.

"We'll find a middle ground," I say.

"I have no doubt," she replies seriously. She takes a sip of tea. "Did you get 'Solicitude'?"

I reach for the painting and hold it up in front of the screen.

"It's good to see it," she says.

"But it's the last time I want to go out there," I reply, "so it's going to stay here with me."

"I like the thought that it's with you."

The most extensive conversation we've had in quite a while. Usually we barely pronounce words. We engage in the nonsense prattle of lovers, a kind of harmonizing like whale song. Some days I can't remember a single thing we've said. Today our call ends with the two of us flinging silly kisses at each other. I sit a while longer at my desk. I feel her absence; I feel my yearning.

My gaze wanders over the "Solicitude" painting. The child, the fountain, the gushing water, the birds. Unconsciously, I have come to think its real title is "Solitude."

PATRICK PFISTER is the author of the novels *American Sadhu* and *North Beach Hotel*, as well as the short story collection, *Far from Home*, all published by Spuyten Duyvil. He has also written two books of travel literature: *Pilgrimage: Tales from the Open Road* and *Over Sand & Sea*, and a book of poetry, *El Camino & Other Travel Poems*. He is the director of two award-winning documentary films: *The Stone Circle* and *Poetry, New York*. He lives in Barcelona, Spain.

patrickpfister.com

www.ingramcontent.com/pod-product-compliance
Lightning Source LLC
Chambersburg PA
CBHW021320190726
48288CB00003B/888